A Dragon's Story

By

Ronny Whitman

Ronny Whitman

Prologue

Dragons. What do we truly know of them?

Do they live, or did they once live? Dragons appear throughout history, whispered in legend and etched into stories passed down through time. Were they creatures of a distant age, survivors from before history was ever written? Or were they tales created to inspire fear, warnings meant to keep those who wished harm at bay?

Many have fantasized about the existence of dragons and wondered what it might have been like to live during an age when such beings ruled the skies. Living, breathing creatures of fire and magic, placed upon this world not to destroy mankind, but to guide and protect it. Powerful. Ancient. Eternal.

Fantasy, some would say. A longing born of imagination and hope. Yet perhaps fantasy is not invention at all, but memory. Truths buried beneath centuries of loss and forgotten time.

For there was a world before history, before mankind recorded its own existence. A time when magic flowed freely and powerful beings walked the land. A time long after the great Ice Age, when druids and magical creatures lived together in harmony, and the age of dragons had not yet faded into legend.

In a time long ago, before history was recorded and during a time after the great Ice Age, where druids and magical creatures existed together in harmony.

The Fae – Fairies, who existed, were the greatest and one of the most powerful creatures that lived on the planet, which was known to them as Terra. They came to this land after their own world was destroyed, blown out of existence, and when they arrived on Terra, it too had been destroyed – the land by a great Ice that seemed to cover most of the planet. Once they landed and disbanded their ships, they sent their people across the planet to repair – healing everything to what it once was, before the big Ice fell. In the process, they discovered a great species – large and powerful creatures that survived when all else was destroyed. Dragons, are what they called them since they were able to spill fire from their mouths, and there were hundreds, possibly thousands of them, and they contained magic like the fae and the fairies, but different.

When the fae queen heard of these magnificent beasts, she immediately sent her most trusted advisors to speak with the dragons, to see if they would be willing to form a friendship that will allow them to both exist in harmony, and when her advisors returned, she was pleased with what she learned.

"They are willing to meet with me," Queen Allabella asked again.

"Aye, Yer Majesty, they are as interested in us as we are in them."

"Then send word to the leader of the dragons and ask them if they would be willing to meet with me in a fourth night, at a place of their choosing."

Aife did not like this idea and as he bowed, "My Queen, should we naught pick the place? Tis would be better to protect ye if we chose the place to meet."

"Aife, I understand yer concern, but we are on their planet and must respect them in ways by giving them the choice," Queen Allabella said. "We want to make friends, not enemies. I am sure they are as curious about us as we are about them. Once we do this, we can open portals to other planets and realms that wish to make a new home here on Terra."

"My Queen, why do ye call this Terra?" Aife asked.

Queen Allabella smiled, "I can feel the energy – vibration of this planet and she whispers to me that her name is Terra."

"Ah, aye, My Queen."

"Now, Aife, go and arrange the meeting with the dragons."

Aife bowed, "as ye wish, My Queen."

Aife turned and left the queen's tent they erected where the fairies built her palace and sent five scouts to deliver the queen's message to the leader of the dragons.

When the scouts arrived at the place where the dragon's resided, and the first dragon they saw, they requested to meet with the leader of the dragons, which turned out to be an ancient dragon, elected because he was the oldest living dragon among them. He would lead the others until he chose to leave this world for the next. Dragons were like the fae – fairies, they could live forever – immortals.

Bran and Ennis were taken to a large cavern where they were introduced to the ancient dragon, and out of respect, Bran and Ennis bowed as they said, "My Lord, tis a pleasure to meet ye."

"Thou are very welcome," said the ancient in his strong rough hoarse voice.

"I bring ye a message from our Queen Allabella. She wishes to make friendship with ye, as we are new to this world."

"Come then, I will bring thy request to the rest of the dragons and see what my kin think about thy idea?"

Surprised and nervous to go in front of so many dragons, Bran asked, "My Lord, are ye no the one to make the decision?"

The ancient smiled, "I am, but my decision will be after I consult with all the dragons, as nay decision is made without the approval of all. Although I have been elected the leader, we dragons together will decide."

Bran turned to look at the other fae that was with him and together agreed to trust the dragon since they could not sense any ill intent coming from the ancient.

When they arrived at the place where all the dragons were gathered, there weren't just a few, but hundreds, possibly thousands of dragons, and Bran and the rest of the Fae became uncomfortable. Yes, they were immortal, but the breath of a dragon could possibly destroy them, and to ensure no harm would come to them, they increased their senses and if they sensed any danger, they could use their power of invisibility to escape. So, once they were in range, Bran and the others increased their senses but felt no threat from the dragons. Instead, the dragons were as interested in them, as they were in the dragons, as the fae were different from what the dragons have ever seen in their long lives.

These Fae, they called themselves, have pointed ears, long smooth silky hair, and their eyes were unlike the dragons had ever seen, as they seem to change color, and from what the dragon could detest, they changed based on their mood, and right now they were silver with a splash of white – fear, is what it was, but then they flashed to a fire orange-red – danger, ready to strike if need be.

Dragons, be alert. I sense fear, yet danger as well. If we give them a reason, thy will attack, but I no naught what power thy have to harm us, the ancient said in the mind of all the dragons.

With this, the dragons began to form a protective circle around the newcomers, which caused Ennis and Bran to become even more uncomfortable with the situation.

We must be cautious, even though we sense no threat, tis can change, said Ennis in Bran's mind.

Ye...we must trust these dragons. Tis be friends of the fae and fairies, tis would be a good alliance, said Bran.

Aye, tis so, but we must be cautious.

Aye, we will.

As the fae's were standing in the center of the dragon's cavern, the ancient one introduced them, and they were wonderfully surprised when all the dragons welcomed them to this new land and planet.

"Our queen will be very pleased, and to celebrate our new friendship, she will want to plan a grand celebration once her castle is complete."

"Castle," the ancient asked, "do thy think we will all fit in thy castle?" he asked with a laugh.

Bran smiled, "aye, ye will. As ye, we have great powers, with the queen more than the rest, as she can expand her castle to accommodate ye, unless ye prefer the outdoors?"

The ancient dragon was surprised to hear this. "Magic, thou have magic?"

Bran smiled, "aye, we do."

"We have not heard of other creatures that have magic like us."

"Forgive me ancient one, but what shall I call ye? Do ye have a name?"

The dragon grinned bearing all of his teeth, "I do, but thou cannot pronounce it, but thee may give me a name of your tongue?"

Bran turned and looked at Ennis, *it must be a great name, one of power for such a beast as he,* said Ennis. *Alasdair.*

"Ye shall be called Alasdair, which means defender of men," Bran said, bowing to Alasdair.

The ancient smiled, "I accept. Thou give me a fine name. From this day forward, I shall be known to thee as Alasdair."

This intrigued the other dragons, and they too wanted a name given to them by the fae, so one by one, Bran and Ennis gave each dragon their own Gaelic name.

On the following morning, Bran and Ennis left the dragon's nest and started their return to their queen with the good news.

"Queen Allabella will be pleased the dragons accepted her offer of friendship," Bran said.

"Aye, she will. They will be able to provide her with much information about this new land."

"Aye, I believe so, as well as other things."

When Bran and Ennis returned to the place they chose as home, they were amazed to see the queen's castle was already complete. It was magnificent, made in a cone shape with colorful crystals spurting out from all around. The small fairies were hard at work, as everything around them was green with beautiful flowers and large, massive trees as far as the eye could see. The castle was surrounded by a large body of water with a crystal bridge and gate, which was the only way to access the castle. There were four guards, two on each side. It was a wonderful place from the one they saw when they first arrived on Terra – alive and vibrant once again.

As Bran and Ennis walked through the gate and into the palace, it was magnificent. The ceilings were as high as the eye could see with an open roof, but then the roof began to close, *fascinating,* Bran thought. As they walked the castle's crystal floor, with each step they took the floor lit up with various colors along with the sound of the fairies, which was a soft hum, a sign a fairy was nearby. Once they arrived at the queen's court, they requested to speak to Queen Allabella with news they bring from the dragons, and when they were granted permission to enter the queen's throne room and were a few feet from the queen, they bowed, "Yer Majesty, we bring ye grand news."

"Well, what news do ye bring me," Queen Allabella asked.

"The dragons have accepted yer friendship and returns there's as well."

"Well then, ye must send word a celebration will commence in a fourth night."

"Aye, Yer Majesty, I will do so immediately."

"Very good. Ye may leave me now."

"As ye wish My Queen," Bran said, and with Ennis, they both bowed, then turned and left.

The day of the celebration between dragon and fae – fairies, was a celebration like no other. With the dragon magic along with fae magic, they created the most amazing celebration, with dragons flying in the sky creating a stream of light as they blasted fireballs across the sky, while the fairies created a light show on the land causing the flowers and trees to dance to the beautiful music they created. Tiny fairies were using their light to create dancing fire in the sky and the dragons helped with this by using their magic to enhance the fire dance and added mini dragons flying in between the dancing fire. It was a beautiful sight to behold.

The fairies were surprised to learn the dragons don't like their meat raw but well cooked, and they don't eat those they call friends, which the fae and fairies were relieved to hear. However, since the great ice fell covering the land and killing most of the animals, food was scarce, which forced the dragons to travel across the land to see if there was a place that wasn't affected by the freeze, and when they did, it took a great deal to bring back the food to the rest of the dragons. When Alasdair learned the queen and her people could produce food with their magic, he knew their alliance would be a great one.

"Alasdair, will ye allow me to read yer soul?" Queen Allabella asked.

When Alasdair first saw Queen Allabella, she was unlike the others. She was taller than most of the fae, with very long black silky hair where the top sat high on the top of her head and flowed down her back and past her waist. Her skin was white, which sparkled with little bits of light, and when she moved, she moved with such grace while producing a soft hum – music. Her eyes were a light blue, which appeared to have a sparkle of light. There was no doubt, she was the most beautiful creature the dragons have beheld.

Alasdair turned to Queen Allabella, "read my soul?" he asked with confusion. "Why would thou want to do so?"

"I have many gifts, and one is to see the past life of a being. It will allow me to see yer life as it was and even further, to lives ye lived before."

"Forgive me, but what reason do thou feel the need to do this?"

"We fae, do no trust easy. Although ye have shown no reason for us to no trust ye, tis would go a long way in our trust if ye would allow me to do so?"

Alasdair watched the queen for a long moment thinking about what she asked, and after a few moments, he decided there was no harm in her request. "Your Majesty, thou have my permission."

Queen Allabella smiled and without further words, she placed her hand on Alasdair's arm and closed her eyes, and what she saw was a being of pure heart and soul, who has lived longer than even she, and she's been alive for many millennia. She saw how they lived before the ice and the beings who once occupied this land, and she was amazed to see they lived in harmony. She also saw other beasts, larger and more deadly, but she also saw ones that were kind and good. The dragons did not harm the people who lived on Terra, although they were ignorant, they lived in peace.

"Ye are what ye say ye are. Ye live with the inhabitants on this planet in peace and fed those beasts ye could, and ye cooked yer meat, unlike the other beast that lived. Yer power is great and old, older than even me, and I am quite old," she said with a smile. "If ye are willing, will ye help me with something? Something I believe with yer power and mine can return man and woman to this land."

"Your Majesty, what would thou ask of me? If it does no harm to another being, I am willing to help thee."

"There are other realms and planets filled with beings of all kinds. The ones I wish to bring to this land are druids. They are also powerful beings with magic of their own, that keep and protect the land. There are planets with beasts that can help populate this land with enough food to serve yer needs."

Alasdair raised his eye, "is what thou say so?" he asked.

"Aye, if ye are willing, aye. If ye wish proof, I will allow ye to touch my mind."

"Thou know I can read thy mind?" he asked with surprise.

Queen Allabella smiled, "aye," was all she said.

"If what thou say is true, then I am willing to help thee."

"This pleases me. We can do this when the moon is high in the sky."

"I will be there. Do thou need many dragons or just me?" Alasdair asked.

"Only I and ye are all is needed. With our powers together, we can open the doorway to other realms and planets. Alasdair, once this is done, would ye be willing to sign a compact between our people and the new people that will come?"

Alasdair touched Queen Allabella's mind, to see if what she says is true, then said, "yes. An agreement between us will be agreeable and assure our friendship for many years. One that will last through time."

"Aye, then on the next moon, we shall meet here at my castle, in my crystal chamber. Tis a chamber covered with the most powerful crystals from my planet, along with ones I found on this planet that will enhance our powers."

"Will I fit in thy castle?" he asked with a raised eye.

Queen Allabella smiled, "I can adjust it for ye."

"Then on the next moon, we will open thy realms and repopulate this planet to thrive once again."

Queen Allabella and her fairies, along with Alasdair and his dragons celebrated until the sun rose on the next day when they departed and returned to their homes.

When the moon was high in the sky, Alasdair arrived at the castle and saw there was a section of the castle that was open in the roof, large enough for him to fly through.

Sensing Alasdair was near, *Alasdair, enter through the roof. It will bring ye directly into the crystal chamber,* said Queen Allabella in his mind.

As Alasdair entered through the roof, the entire chamber was filled with crystals of all sizes, and he could feel their vibrations – they seemed to be speaking to him – welcoming him. Once he landed, he bowed his head, "Your Majesty, tis a pleasure to see thou again."

Although she would not do this to any other, Queen Allabella curtsied to Alasdair, showing respect to a great ancient and leader of all dragons as he. "Ye are very welcome."

Once Queen Allabella and Alasdair were standing in the center of the crystal room, Alasdair was surprised at how the room expanded to accommodate his large frame, and with the roof open, it also allowed them direct access to the power of the full moon. The crystal room was made of several colorful crystals that seemed to vibrate with a soft hum, the same sound generated by the queen when she moved.

"Thou have made a communication chamber, allowing thee to communicate far and wide and across the stars. Where did thou acquire these many crystals?" Alasdair asked.

"Ye know of this? How?" she asked, then explained how she came by so many crystals. "I brought many with me when I left my home world, but many we found here on Terra."

"I know of this from the memories the last ancient bestowed on me before he left this world," he said, then, "how did thy learn of their location?" he asked. He knew of the crystals because the planet spoke to him of the power they contain, but he never had the need to use them.

Queen Allabella smiled, "the planet speaks to me as well," she said.

"Ah, My Lady, thee reads minds as well," he said with amusement.

"Aye, tis true," she said with laughter.

"What will thou do next to open the doorway to these other realms?"

"See the center crystals?" Queen Allabella said, pointing to the center console. Alasdair nodded. "Ye stand on one side, and I will stand on the other. We need to focus our mind and energy on those crystals, and I will say the words that will open the doorway to the realm of light, which will allow the druids to enter this realm."

Alasdair did as Queen Allabella requested, "and we will look up to thy moon to draw down its power to enhance ours," he said, reading Allabella's mind.

Queen Allabella smiled, "tis so. Now, we will begin. Take the words from my mind and say them at the same time I do."

"As thy wish."

And together they said the words, "tese maete pata naete tato maca chenu mate pata mae te. tese maete pata naete tato maca chenu mate pata maete. tese maete pata naete tato maca chenu mate pata mae te." Repeating the words over and over again, chanting until they saw a shimmer in the center crystals and they began to glow, followed by a crack that revealed a door, and after a few moments, the door completely opened and someone from the other side spoke.

"My Queen, do we have your permission to enter your realm?"

"Aye, ye have my permission, enter at will."

And ten men and women dressed in gold hooded robes entered the crystal chamber, and once they were through, Alasdair and Queen Allabella stopped chanting, allowing the door to close, then turned towards the newcomers and bowed their heads showing respect to the druids.

"Ye are very welcome to this new planet called Terra. This," directing her attention to Alasdair, "is Alasdair, a dragon living on this planet."

A man stepped forward, who appeared to be the leader of the group, "it is a pleasure to meet such an ancient," said the man bowing to Alasdair. "Your kind have been well known and respected by our people for many years."

This surprised Alasdair, "thou know of my kind?" he asked.

"Yes, we knew of your kind when you first arrived on this planet and chose to make it your home."

This surprised Alasdair and Queen Allabella, "this is no yer first time on this planet?" Queen Allabella asked.

The man smiled, "no, it is not."

"Thou know of my kind?" Alasdair asked.

"Yes, from when your kind first came to this planet."

"How did ye arrive then?" Queen Allabella asked.

"The ancient of that time had the power to open the door to our realm, but it appears he did not share that information with the one who took his place," he said looking at Alasdair.

Alasdair was surprised of the ancient before him, who knew of the druids, and wondered why he chose not to share this information with him before he transcended to the next world.

"It might be because he didn't believe you would have need for us, and it appears he was right. Your kind has lived a long and prosperous life, even after the great ice fell," said the druid leader.

"Thou can read minds as well," Alasdair said, but without waiting for an answer, he went on, "no, we had no need, but we had no knowledge of thee. Tis been hard for us to survive after the ice fell, but we managed. If we knew of thee, we may have reached out to thee for help."

The leader druid smiled, "no, I do not think you would have. You are too proud and believe you can survive any obstacle, which you have already proven."

"Druid, what is thy name?"

"My name is Cathbad. I am at your service ancient one," he said bowing to Alasdair.

"Thou is Cathbad, "Alasdair said with surprise. "I have heard thy name before. Spoken by the ancient one before me and he heard it from the one before him. I wonder why thou was not spoken of to he."

"Alasdair," said Queen Allabella, "in what manner did ye hear this name?" she asked.

Alasdair searched his memory in how the name Cathbad was spoken, and when he found it, "thou name was spoken of an ancient one who helped see our people to this land. We believed it was a dragon they spoke of though."

"Did they mention anything else?" asked Queen Allabella.

"If thou in need of Cathbad, thou only have to reach to the stars and think of his name and Cathbad will appear."

"Tis simple, and yet ye no call for him," asked Queen Allabella.

"I had no reason to. How can dragons call on thee when it took the power of Queen Allabella and my energy to bring thee here?

"You have the power in you. You and all the dragons together can call on me."

Amazed by this, as well as fascinated their kind had such powers that they were unaware of.

"Come, there is much to discuss and prepare for," said Cathbad.

For the next several moons, the druids, dragons, and fairies worked to build a village and create food from the land around them, and together they created animals of various kinds to feed all man, woman, and creature, and once they were done, there was a thriving village, and it was time for Cathbad to return to the realm of light.

Cathbad called forth other druids who wished to live on Terra, and when the door opened for him to leave, hundreds of druids came through to make a life in the new world. However, there was a disadvantage to them living on Terra, the powers they had in the realm of light would diminish over time, and when that time came, Cathbad or one like him would return and choose one druid to be the leader of all druids, and the one they choose would have to prove they were pure of heart and soul for them to possess the power of the druids, as it will be for each generation thereafter.

Chapter 1

A thousand years later, Terra's population grew dramatically with druids, dragons, fae, and fairies, and they all lived together in peace and harmony. Alasdair decided after five hundred years that he lived long enough and was ready to transcend to the next world and his position was given to the next ancient who was called Beladore, who continued with the way things were in honor of the great ancient dragon.

"Mate, what are thou doing?"

"I am resting. What does thou need of me?"

"For thee to fly with me."

"Nay, why do thou lay with me instead."

"What is wrong Darca?" Tlachtga asked with a more serious tone.

Sighing, "I feel lonely and sad. I know naught why."

Tlachtga laid down beside his mate, "Darca, why do thou feel this way?"

Darca closed her eyes and rested her head on her claws, "I know naught. I feel…I am missing something."

"Thou is my mate, am I not enough?"

Squeezing her eyes tight, "thou is my mate, my love, but thou…I want more."

"Love, tell me what thou want," he asked rubbing his head against hers.

"I want," sighing, "I want children."

Tlachtga laughed, then moved closer to his mate, "thou only need to ask, and thou shall have children.

Darca was surprised, "thou never said thee wanted children."

"How can I naught want children," he said, then took his mate and pulled her into an embrace as he took them to

17

the sky, high above the clouds so they would not be seen, where Tlachtga made love to his mate and seeded her eggs.

"Now mate, thee will have my children."

Darca felt content as she felt her eggs being seeded by her mate. Sighing, "thee have given me a great gift."

"Thee are my gift and our children will be the best of both of us."

Darca smiled, feeling happy knowing their children were growing inside of her. "Thou know when the time comes to lay my eggs, I will have to go to sleep until they are ready to hatch. Will thee be alright without me?"

"Thee are my heart. If I must spend several moons without thee for our children to be born, I will do my best to be without thee during that time. Thee will be very much missed though," Tlachtga said, rubbing his head against Darca's neck.

"When the sun is high I will tell Queen Allabella that she will have to find an advisor for the time I am asleep."

"She will miss thee."

Darca smiled, "she will. Since our time together, she and I have become great friends."

"She will be happy for thee."

"Yes, she will be. Come, let us return to our cave and rest."

Together Daca and Tlachtga returned to the cave they shared that was located high above the clouds.

Darca was chosen long ago to become Queen Allabella's trusted advisor of the dragons, a great honor to be given to a dragon, and as they worked together, they formed a great friendship.

"Darca, Queen Allabella has requested thy presents."

18

"I will go to her at once," she said, and without delay, she headed to the castle. *I will tell her my good news,* she thought as she flew into the queen's throne room.

Queen Allabella smiled when she saw Darca. When she selected Darca to become her advisor for the dragons, she never imagined they would become close friends. She, a queen, was friends with no one, but this dragon, there was something about her – she felt a kinship with Darca. Maybe because she was the daughter of her former advisor, Alasdair, she wasn't sure, nor has she asked to see into her soul to find out.

"Darca, tis always a pleasure to see ye."

"Your Majesty, as thou is for me," Darca said bowing her head.

"Darca, ye no need to bow to me. I have told ye this before."

"Yes, Your Majesty, this is done out of respect for thee."

"Can I no change thy mind then?"

"Nay, Your Majesty."

"Can I no have ye call me Allabella?"

"Nay, thou is not proper."

"Very well. Come, let us talk."

"As you wish Your Majesty."

"Darca, I have heard there are problems with the fae that live on the north side of the planet. It is said they are using and abusing their power against men and women by forcing them to serve them as slaves, and if they refuse, they are killed or worse, they are cursed, and in some cases, their families too.

"This is horrible news, Your Majesty. What can thy do to stop this?"

"I want ye to take me to where this is happening so I can see for myself that the news is true."

"Your Majesty, thou have the ability to go without my help."

"Aye, but they will know I am coming when they feel my power. I no want them to know I am coming. I am going to change my appearance so I can blend in with the regular people, which will allow me to see the truth."

"Then I will do as thy wish and join thee in disguise. As thou know I can change into a form of my choosing."

"Aye, I have heard of this, but I have no seen it for myself."

Just then, Darca transformed into a female fae. "What do thou think?"

Queen Allabella was amazed by the transformation, and there was very little that amazed her anymore. "Ye make a beautiful fae, and ye can do this for any species?"

"Yes, I need only to see their form and then I can copy it."

"Will ye be ready at sunrise on the morrow?"

"As thou wish, Your Majesty."

"Now, will ye take meal with me in fae form?"

Darca smiled, "I will be honored."

Darca and Queen Allabella had a wonderful time together and she informed Queen Allabella of her great news.

"How wonderful news!" Queen Allabella said with excitement. "How long before ye lay yer eggs and go to sleep?"

"In six moons."

"So soon," Queen Allabella said with sadness.

"Yes, Your Majesty."

"Ye will be very much missed. Will thee recommend a dragon to take yer place? Ye know I trust yer opinion."

Darca smiled, "I may have one in mind, but I must speak with them first."

"Very well. I will wait to hear who ye choose."

Darca and Queen Allabella continued their time together and when it was time for Darca to leave, she turned back to her dragon form and returned to her mate.

At sunrise, Darca met Queen Allabella at the back of the castle. She landed in the meadow that was surrounded by large trees, filled with plants and a wonderful mixture of colorful flowers that were spread far and wide, and in the far corner was a large pond filled with large lilies.

"Good morrow, Darca."

"Good morrow, Queen Allabella," Darca said as she bowed her head.

Queen Allabella smiled, *can I no get her to call me Allabella,* she thought shaking her head.

"It is not proper My Queen."

Sighing, "very well."

Just then, Draca produced a saddle on her back for Queen Allabella, and the queen transformed into a human female, then floated up and situated herself on the saddle Darca provided. Once Queen Allabella was ready, Darca took to the sky and flew north, and once they were near their destination, Darca made them invisible so they would not be seen and landed in a forest just outside the village. After Darca and Queen Allabella was sure no one was around, Queen Allabella floated down to the ground and then Darca transformed into a human as well, before becoming visible again.

Ronny Whitman

"We will walk to the village and move among the people to get a feel for what is happening," said Queen Allabella.

"Very well. Do thee feel what I am feeling?" Darca asked.

"Aye, fear. A great deal of fear. Let us go and see what we can learn."

When Darca and Queen Allabella reached the village, they found a thriving village with people bustling around. From the outside, they could not find anything wrong, but fear was prevalent in the air. Darca and Queen Allabella made their way to the village inn and went inside to take a room since they didn't know how long they would need to stay.

"Good day," said the innkeeper.

"Good day," said Darca and Queen Allabella.

"Do you wish for a room?"

"Yes," said Queen Allabella, changing her speech to the one the locals used.

"Just one room?" asked the innkeeper.

"Yes, with two beds if you have it," said Darca.

"Your names?" asked the innkeeper.

Darca turned to Queen Allabella, *we need to use different names,* said Queen Allabella in Darca's mind.

"I am Mary and this," motioning with her hand, "is Sophie," Queen Allabella said.

"Wonderful. How many nights will you be staying?" he asked motioning for a girl that was washing the floors. "Jane, take Mary and Sophie to their room." Turning back to Mary and Sophie, "do you wish to have a meal brought to your room?"

Mary and Sophie looked at each other, "we are unsure of how many days we will need. If we can pay day by day

Ronny Whitman

as needed? Yes, a meal would be wonderful after our long journey," said Mary (Queen Allabella).

"That will not be a problem. Very well, I will bring it straight away."

The girl took Queen Allabella and Darca to their rooms and once they were inside and the door was closed, "well, after we eat we will walk the village to see what we can discover."

"As you wish Your…Mary," Darca said.

Queen Allabella smiled, *ye are forced to call me by my name, but no my name.*

Darca smiled, *as thou knew I would.*

Once the innkeeper delivered their meal, Darca and Queen Allabella ate in silence, and once finished, they headed out of the inn and to the village. At first, everything looked normal, and then they saw a male fae with a human female who was wearing a collar with a long chain that was controlled by the fae.

That collar and chain are used to control the human. If they anger the fae, he can send an energy that will cause great pain to the human, and if given enough, can kill the human.

Is there anything thee can do to help the human?

Aye, but no yet. I need to see more.

Just then, one of the merchants turned and bumped into the fae, and the fae snapped his fingers and the merchant disappeared.

What happened to that human?

He has the power to send one to another place or realm. This power is rare and is usually coveted by the fae, but this one has decided to use his power for evil. He could have sent the man anywhere on the planet or to another realm, one that would be harmful to the man.

Ronny Whitman

Can you find the man and return him?

Aye, but no now. If I use my power to do so, I will give myself away.

How long can the man survive wherever he was sent?

I no naught. It depends on where he was sent, but I can no see that now. We must follow that fae to where I am sure there are others and see what else they are up to.

Very well. Shall I cloak us?

No yet, we will follow the fae. We will pretend to be shopping and once the fae is out of the village, we will duck out of sight and then ye can cloak us and follow the fae to where he lives and hope he will lead us to the other fae's.

Queen Allabella and Darca followed the fae and what they saw was disturbing. Anyone the fae came across that he did not like, he caused harm or did something of mischief – causing a human to trip and fall on their face, and a male human to punch another male human, causing a fight, and many more.

When the fae was finally out of the village and far enough away and out of sight of any humans, Darca cloaked them both, as they continued to follow the evil fae who led them to a large structure where, from what Queen Allabella could sense, were many evil fae's congregating together.

What can thy do to stop this? Darca asked.

Ah, my friend, I can do this, Queen Allabella said as she approached and entered the door to the structure where the Fae was, and when she walked across the threshold, she was no longer the human called Mary, but the powerful Queen Allabella, ruler of the fae. "Good afternoon," she said.

When Queen Allabella spoke, she spoke with such power all the fae turned with fear in their eyes. One male fae, who appeared to be the leader spoke, "ye, what are ye doing here?" he asked with a stutter.

"Apparently to punish fae who are breaking the law against humans," Queen Allabella said with anger and a force of power that shook the building. "By the law of the fae and the agreement with the humans, I punish ye to death!" she roared.

"No Yer Majesty. We did no harm, only what was required to do so. These humans have caused great harm to our people, and they had to be punished," one fae said.

"Nae, tis is no the truth. Ye dare lie to yer queen?"

"My Queen, please, we did no harm, but what was required," another fae pleaded.

"If tis so, then ye no mine me reading each, and every one of yer minds for proof?"

All of the fae's looked at each other and knew if she did what she said, she would know the truth. So, they decided to do what Queen Allabella expected them to do. It was what she presumed was the leader who made the first strike, but Queen Allabella deflected the strike and with a thought, she destroyed all the evil fae. However, unknown to her, a couple of evil fae managed to escape out back.

"Queen Allabella, could thy not help them instead of destroying them?"

"Nae Darca. These were very evil fae, nothing I would have done or said would have stopped them from hurting humans. Now, I will restore all the humans they harmed, cursed, and made disappear from this world. What ye do no know Darca, is I was reading their minds and they had no intention of changing. They believed I should not have any Authority over them and were planning to remove me as queen by taking my life."

Darca was amazed by Queen Allabella's power and her ability to touch a mind without the other knowing. She watched as Queen Allabella left the building and traveled back to the village, to seek the human minds that were controlled by the fae and returned their minds to what it was before. For the ones that disappeared, she took that information from the evil fae's before she destroyed them, and with a thought, they all returned from where they were removed, and all was well between humans and fae once more. However, those fae's who escaped would go into hiding until the day they believed it was safe to resurface, and again try to destroy the humans and Queen Allabella.

"It is time for us to return home," said Queen Allabella, and with that, Darca returned to her dragon form, and together they returned home.

Several days later, Talchtga and Darca were flying through the night sky beneath the bright moon and stars. It was a magical night for them both. Darca knew her time has come to lay her eggs and she would go into a deep sleep until they were ready to hatch. Talchtga knew this day would come, but he was not ready to let her go, not yet, so he convinced her to have this one last night together flying beneath the moon and stars.

"Will thou race me?" Talchtga asked.

"Why do thou ask me, thy know I will beat thee," Darca said with a laugh.

"Thou may beat me, but thou will naught know unless thou try?" Talchtga said with mockery.

"Then thou shall race me?"

Darca nodded her head, and with that, Talchtga took off before she knew it. Shocked, "thou cheat to beat me," she said as she sped to catch up with him, but she didn't just catch up, she passed him with flying speed, thus winning the race. "Although thou cheat, thee could not beat me."

"Nay, I only wanted to see thee, who is so powerful, beat me," Talchtga said with laughter before he took her in a tight embrace, and they made love above the clouds.

Later, exhausted from making love, "thou know it is time for me to sleep. I will miss thee," whispered Darca.

"Not as much as I will miss thee."

After lying together for a few more minutes, Talchtga went with Darca to where she created her nest, and once she was asleep, Talchtga left her and returned to the others.

When Talchtga arrived at the large dragon cavern, he noticed the dragons were restless, concerned about something.

"Beladore, can thou tell me what is amiss?" Talchtga asked.

"One of the dragons who have the foresight has seen great balls of fire fall from the sky destroying everything in its path."

"This can naught be? I just left Darca asleep with our eggs until they are ready to hatch."

"Nay worry. I will have Queen Allabella erect a protection shield until the danger is over and she is ready to wake."

"I must go to her and rest by her side until that day comes."

"Nay, I will need thee here with the other dragons to help the fae and fairies place safeguards around us and all of the humans."

Although Talchtga wanted to return to Darca, Beladore was right – their agreement with humans and fairies must be honored. So, for the next few days, the dragons and fairies did everything they could to protect as many of the people, dragons, and fairies along with saving as many of the animals and plant life around them, and by the time this was done, Talchtga barely had time to return to Darca, where he laid by her side before the great balls of fire fell from the sky.

It had continued to rain fire for three moons before it finally stopped, and the destruction it caused was more than they expected. It took six moons for the dragons and fairies to heal the planet. For the people, well, many survived, but many died when some of the protection shields failed. A loss that will haunt Queen Allabella for many years. For Darca, although Tlachtga stayed by her side for many moons, eventually he was forced to leave her side and return to the other dragons to help heal Terra, but what Tlachtga didn't know, was the magic that protected her, placed her in a deep sleep that no amount of magic used would awaken her, which left Tlachtga heartbroken and for Queen Allabella, a loss of a good and loyal friend.

Many thousands of years had passed, and during that time, the two evil fae's that escaped Queen Allabella managed to form a new group and called themselves the Unseelie Fae who worked to destroy the Seelie Fae and Queen Allabella. In this, the power to control all the fae was at risk and both fractions were forced to a new realm they called the Fairy Realm. In this, Queen Allabella managed to control the Unseelie Fae and exiled them to a place on the Fairy Realm with a protection shield preventing them from interacting with the Seelie Fae and any access to return to the human realm.

For the dragons, they continued their path to help and protect the humans, until one day, in the 1100s, when a dragon called Cillian who partnered with a wizard called Dornazi, who practiced the dark arts, turned against the other dragons and the agreement with the humans. Cillian believed since they had great power and were larger and stronger than humans, that dragons should rule over humans, but Beladore, the ancient dragon and leader of all the dragons did not agree, and the agreement made long ago between the dragon, fae, fairy, and humans would be honored. If a dragon would go against the agreement, Beladore would be forced, with great resistance, put that dragon to death. But Cillian did not see it that way, and one day found a human soldier who he felt he could manipulate, bend to his will, and destroy humans and dragons, leaving only himself to rule the humans in the world of Terra.

"Beladore, Cillian is working with the Anglo-Saxons to destroy villages and killing humans in the process and blaming it on us dragons," said Tlachtga.

Sighing, "we have given Cillian many times to bend to the agreement we have with the humans, and I am afraid I will have to do something no dragon has ever done. I will have to put Cillian to death," Beladore said with great sadness in his heart.

No dragon has ever betrayed another dragon, and for this one dragon, Cillian to betray all dragons, there was only one recourse – death.

"Are thy sure this is our only option? Can we naught change his way of thinking?" asked Tlachtga.

"Cillian has already been given many chances, and still, he works to destroy us. There is no other option. There is a wizard called Merlin, I believe can assist us with this."

"I am aware of this wizard and agree he could be of great help."

"Then I will send word to him, and ask him to meet with me, so we can make a plan to capture Cillian and then…with heavy heart…put him to death."

"As thou must," said Tlachtga with sadness.

Beladore and Tlachtga called for the wizard Merlin, and in two days he arrived at the cave where Beladore and the other dragons resided.

"Merlin, tis a pleasure to see thee again," said Beladore.

"And thee," Merlin said bowing.

"How was thou journey?" asked Tlachtga.

"Journey was well, thank thee Tlachtga. Now tell me, what is thy plan to stop Cillian?"

"I believe tis best if we combine our power to put Cillian into a deep sleep, one he would not wake from without our powers," said Beladore.

"If thou can naught capture and put him to sleep?" Merlin asked.

"Then, we must combine our power to destroy Cillian once and for all," said Beladore.

Surprised by this, "thee has never killed a dragon before," said Merlin.

With heavy heart, "nay, not as long as I am aware, but there may be no choice," said Beladore.

Beladore, Tlachtga, and Merlin, together went in search of Cillian, and no matter the combination of all their powers, they could not stop him, who to their shock, had been practicing black magic which made it very difficult to trap him, and now, the only option they had was to destroy Cillian once and for all, and the only way they could do that was to call on the fae queen to assist.

30

Merlin, along with Beladore summoned the fae queen and requested her permission to open the door so she may enter the human realm. Once they received their answer agreeing to allow the door to be opened, Beladore and Merlin didn't waste time in opening the door and once the queen entered, "thou is welcome to Terra," said Beladore as he, Tlachtga, and Merlin bowed.

Queen Allabella turned to Tlachtga, "tis a pleasure to see thee again Tlachtga. How are ye and Darca?" she asked and did not miss the sadness that crossed Tlachtga's face. "Tell me, what is wrong?" she asked.

Shaking his head, "forgive me Queen Allabella, but Darca has been lost to us forever."

"How can this be? Have ye no try magic to waken her again?"

"We did every twelve moons, to no avail," Tlachtga said with sadness.

"This can no be?" Queen Allabella said with surprise and sadness. "Well, once we take care of this evil dragon, we will try again using all of our powers, including Merlin's. Maybe with all our powers, we can awaken Darca."

With hope in his heart, "thou may be right. We did not have the wizard's power before."

"I will be more than happy to help thee return thy love and children to thee," said Merlin.

"So, tell me about this evil dragon?" Queen Allabella asked.

"Your Majesty, he is a new dragon born only a thousand years ago, and we do not know what went wrong, but I believe he was born with evil in his blood. Since he was old enough to understand our ways, he has done everything against our ways and the laws we created. We kept a close watch on him and kept him from harming another, and believed our actions helped change his ways, as he accepted our ways and the laws we created until he was a full-grown dragon and went off on his own. It was many years later when we heard of his mischiefs. At first, they were small, but then grew into two much larger ones. In frightening the humans and causing great destruction, but when he put himself in the hands of the Anglo-Saxons, he started killing humans and destroying villages and making it look like the dragons…all the dragons were at fault. Now humans have turned against us and work to destroy us. We have lost many, and many with young ones have gone into hiding until one day Cillian's reign ends. We must destroy Cillian and remove him from this world for good," said Beladore.

"This is heartening news. I never believed a dragon would do such a thing, but as ye have explained, tis so. I have the power along with all the dragons and," turning to Merlin, "this wizard's power, as I can sense he holds great power from many lifetimes, can and will destroy Cillian for good, but we must act fast. Where can we find Cillian now?" Queen Allabella asked.

"Thou will find him six leagues from here in the Anglo-Saxon camp," said Merlin.

"Then, let us be off," said Queen Allabella.

It took Beladore, Tlachtga, Merlin, and Queen Allabella a day and a half to reach the outer skirts of the Anglo-Saxon camp. They chose to walk, as they did not want to alert Cillian they were coming, and the use of magic would.

"We need to lure Cillian away from the Anglo-Saxons," said Queen Allabella.

"Thy will need me. If I show myself, Cillian will leave the camp to try and capture me. He hates me more than any other. I no naught why," said Beladore.

"Then ye will need to fly and try to destroy the camp, and when Cillian comes after ye, lure him to the open meadow we passed half a league away. Once ye have him there and are engaged in battle, reach us through our mind and we will use our magic to join ye."

Beladore bowed his head, "tis a good plan. I will go at once."

Beladore took to the air and flew over the camp spilling fire and torching a few tents, but only those he knew were empty. The Anglo-Saxon soldiers were spilling out to attack, but when Cillian showed up, he warned the others off, "this is my fight," he yelled and sped towards Beladore, who after spewing fire at Cillian a few times, took off to the meadow.

Once they arrived at the meadow, Beladore tried to reason with Cillian, wanting to do everything to save his life. "Cillian, tis naught too late to return to your brethren and be the dragon I know thou can be."

"Thou can naught return me to thy rules and way of life. I am happier with the freedom I have," Cillian said, then breathed fire at Beladore.

Beladore flew out of the way of Cillian's fire and threw his own fire and scarcely singed Cillian's left wing.

This angered Cillian, "thou will pay for that," he roared and then stopped in midair and began to call on his powers of dark magic."

Now, thee must come now! Cillian is calling on dark magic. And just then, Tlachtga, Merlin, and Queen Allabella appeared in the meadow and together drew magic and formed it around Cillian creating a protective bubble,

33

and with their powers slowly but surely began to tear away Cillian scales one by one. It was a painful process, but one that had to be done to ensure Cillian does not survive. It seemed like a lifetime before he vanished from this world forever.

Once Cillian was gone, Beladore was heartbroken. Never did he believe it was in his power to destroy a dragon, but with Cillian, it had to be done, and this was the only way. "Thank thee for helping me with this, but I must go and rest for many moons," Beladore said. He couldn't bear to face the other dragons, so he decided to go to a place where he would sleep the sleep of dragons until he was ready to rise once again.

"Beladore, must thou. Thou is needed. Thee are our leader," said Tlachtga.

"Nay Tlachtga, I can naught face the others knowing what I have done, and the power I used to destroy him has exhausted me."

"Beladore, ye have great honor. No one will blame ye for what ye had to do, and it was no only ye," turning to the others, "but all of us who destroyed Cillian."

"Yes, I am aware, but…I can not face them, not now," he said with sadness.

"Then my friend, we will not stop thee," Merlin said, putting his hand on Tlachtga as he was about to argue, "this is what he must do, not for us, but for himself. If thee love him, thee must let him go."

Tlachtga nodded his head, "go Beladore, go with honor and when thee awake, we will be here waiting for thee."

Beladore nodded his head and flew north towards the high mountains where he found a cave and burrowed deep inside, and once he felt he was deep enough in the earth, he closed the hole and went to sleep.

"Queen Allabella, do thy think your power along with mine and the rest of the dragons would be enough to awaken Darca?" Tlachtga asked.

"I no naught, but tis possible with Merlin's powers we may be able to, but with Beladore being the dragon with the most power it may no be possible, but we will try," Queen Allabella said looking to Merlin.

"We will try," Merlin said.

Queen Allabella, Tlachtga, Merlin, and the rest of the dragons arrived at Darca's resting place, and Tlachtga and Queen Allabella both reached out to Darca to try and wake her, but there was no response, no hint she was trying to wake.

"Aye, we must put all our powers together and reach for Darca's mind and try to pull her to the surface so she will wake," said Queen Allabella.

The dragon's formed an unbreakable circle around Darca's resting place and Tlachtga, Queen Allabella, and Merlin floated above, and together they used all their powers to try and wake Darca, but no matter how hard they tried, she would not wake.

"Why will she naught wake?" Tlachtga asked.

"I do no understand myself, unless, for some reason, Darca does no want to wake?"

"Nay, I can naught believe this."

"I am sorry Tlachtga, we will have to wait for her to wake when she is ready. What I will do, I will enforce her protection shield, with yer help Merlin, I believe we can make it strong and impenetrable until Darca is ready to wake. When she wakes, the shield will collapse," said Queen Allabella.

Tlachtga lowered his head, "if this is the only way, then thy may do so."

Queen Allabella and Merlin, along with all the dragons help create the shield to protect Darca, and Queen Allabella put that one part in the spell that will lower the shield upon Darca's awakening. "What will ye do now?" Darca asked Tlachtga.

"I do naught know. My life is with Darca. I may go into a deep sleep until she wakes."

"No, tis would no be good. Ye are needed here."

Shaking his head, "nay, there is no reason for me to stay." Turning to the other dragons, "the dragons have decided to go into a deep sleep until it is safe to return. Although Cillian is dead, what he has done, the humans no longer trust the dragons. It is too dangerous for us to remain."

Queen Allabella looked to the others, and they all nodded in agreement, "with Beladore leaving us, our leader, tis best we do the same," said Rollo, one of the younger dragons.

"If tis so, then I will offer any who wish it, may return with me to my realm and when another wizard from the future opens the door, ye will have a choice to return to this realm. For those who wish to return to my realm, come to my side." To Queen Allabella's surprise, there were twenty dragons who formed a circle around her, "well then, Merlin, if ye will open a door big enough for all of us to go through."

"As thee wish." Merlin opened the door creating a shield to protect those on the other side from getting through, but large enough for Queen Allabella and the dragons to enter. "When thee are ready to return, call on me and I will open thy door."

All the dragons that decided to go to the Fairy Realm stepped through the door, leaving Tlachtga and Queen Allabella for last, "Merlin, ye will no be the one to return the dragons, but one far off in the future will open the door to my realm."

"Thou see what I see. A world and time unfamiliar to us both," Merlin said, then turned to Tlachtga, "as will thy Darca.

Tlachtga was surprised by this, "so long then?" he asked.

"Aye, this true Tlachtga, but for ye, it will not be so long. Time in my realm moves differently than this one.

"Then I shall wait for that day when I can be with my Darca once again."

With that, Queen Allabella stepped through the door followed by Tlachtga.

"Well, it appears I have much to prepare for, for this future that is to come," Merlin whispered.

Chapter 2

It was the year 2021 and Ian was at work in his office located in downtown Phoenix working as an accountant for a great company when word came that the Russians had declared war on the United States, England, France, and many other European countries that were under the United Union Agreement.

"Mark, what are we going to do?" Ian asked.

"Man, I have no idea. Do you think Arizona will be in their path of destruction?" Mark asked with concern in his voice.

"I don't know man. I hope not. They will for sure go to Washington D.C., New York, and Pennsylvania."

"Man, are you going to leave Arizona like so many others?"

"No. Why? What would it matter? Where could we go that will protect us? I'd rather stay here and take my chances. How about you?"

"Man, as soon as they close down the office, I am taking my family and heading north to the woods. I believe we will be safe there. You are crazy for staying. You should come with us? You'd be more than welcome."

Ian shook his head, "no man. I'm staying. I have no family…not anymore, and I have no reason to leave. Phoenix is my home, and I will remain here."

Ian remembers his family – his wife and son, how they died in a car accident on the I-10 on their way home from a play at the Phoenix Theater, because of an idiot – a drunk driver who was driving the wrong way on the freeway. Bell and little Ian didn't see it coming. What he takes comfort in, is what the Authorities told him, death was immediate, so they felt no pain. But now, now was not the time for Ian to dwell on the past.

"Attention, attention, the office is closing, and everyone should leave the office and head home to your families and pray the Russians will pass us by. Good luck to you all and may God be with you."

"Well man, that is it. I am off. I wish you luck and that you survive whatever is to come."

"You too Mark."

When Ian arrived home at his apartment in Mesa, he quickly called his parents who lived in New York City, fearing for their safety.

"Ian honey, your father and I will be fine. We are packing and heading to the Hamptons until this is all over."

"Mother, do you think you will be safe in the Hamptons?"

"Yes, darling. The Hamptons is far away from where we feel the Russians will attack."

"Alright, but you must be safe and leave quickly."

"Yes darling, we will. What about you? Where will you go to wait out this danger?"

"I am going to stay in my apartment. I believe I will be safe here."

"Mesa? Aren't you worried you will be in danger there?"

"No mother, as the Russian's main target are the larger cities like Washington. They will target the white house, Pennsylvania for the Pentagon, and New York City, California, and other large metropolitan cities. I think Arizona is the least of their concerns. I will be safe," Ian assured his mother.

Sighing, "I am glad to hear this," his mother said as her attention was drawn away from their conversation when she heard the car was there to pick them up. "Ian dear, the car has arrived, and your father and I must go. We love you, Ian."

"Yes, Ian, we love you, and be safe," said his father. "Come, dear, we must be on our way."

"Yes, of course. Goodbye, Ian."

"Goodbye mother and I love you both," Ian said then disconnected the call.

Shortly after Ian hung up the phone, he heard fighter jets racing toward where he was. Ian quickly went out on the balcony and what he saw would be embedded in his memory for all time. The Russian fighters were racing through, and as they did so, they were dropping bombs and the American fighters were firing bullets at the Russians trying to force them out of the sky. Right in front of Ian, one Russian fighter crashed into a group of stores across the street from his apartment and then another. One crashed right in front of him, nearly hitting his apartment complex.

"I think it's time to leave," he said as he turned and grabbed what he could and ran out the door and to his car, where he found others in the complex doing the same thing. Ian got in his car and when he looked at his gas gauge, he found he only had a half tank, "well, that isn't going to get me far. Will I be able to get gas?" Looking around, "no, there is no time," he said, and just then the gas station blew up. "Nope, no time for that. I will have to just drive and go as far as I can."

Ian decided to head east, out of the city limits and into the desert where there was nothing for the Russians to bomb, and he was right, because once he was out of the city limits, he ended up at a farmhouse, and after a few minutes, he decided to take the chance, so he drove closer to the house, and after a few minutes he went and knocked on the door. When the door opened, there was an old man with a gun in his hand and an old woman standing by his side.

"Who are you?" the old man demanded.

Ian looked at the old man and then down at his hands, the old man was holding a shotgun, but his hands were shaking as if it was too heavy for him.

"You have nothing to fear from me. I am only looking for refuge after escaping the attack in Mesa."

The old man raised the gun, "how do I know you are not a Russian pretending to be an American."

"Sir, if I were a Russian, I would be wearing a Russian uniform. Please, sir, I am not here to harm you, only to seek safety."

"Let him in Bill. He seems harmless," said the old woman.

"I don't know Beth. He could be lying."

"If he was lying, he would have already forced his way in. Let him in Bill."

Bill looked Ian up and down, then after a few moments, he released his breath and stepped aside to let Ian in. "Well, come in boy."

"Thank you, sir. My name is Ian Burrow."

"I am Bill, and this is Beth my wife and you are on Smith Farm."

"Come Ian. Are you hungry?" Beth asked.

Ian didn't realize how hungry he was until that moment, and placed his hand on his stomach, "yes ma'am, I am starved."

"Well then, come into the kitchen and I will fix you something to eat," she said, then turned to her husband, "Bill, put that damn gun away."

Bill, with Ian's help, placed the gun back on its rack. "It wasn't loaded. I haven't used that gun in years."

Ian raised his eyebrow, "if I were a Russian, what would you have done?"

Shrugging his shoulders, "well, I didn't think that far," Bill said.

Ian smiled, "well it was a good thing it was me and not a Russian."

Bill chuckled, "yes well…let us go eat and you can tell me what happened before you arrived."

Over a delicious hot meal, Ian told Bill and Beth about what he witnessed in Mesa before he left. "I don't believe they will come this way. They seemed to be heading towards California."

"Well, that is good to know," said Beth with concern.

"Ian, you are welcome to stay here as long as you want," said Bill.

"Thank you. I am very grateful. Do you have a phone? I would like to call my mother and father. When I last spoke to my mother, they were leaving New York City."

Bill and Beth looked at each other, "Ian, when was the last time you saw the news?" Bill asked.

"I don't know, right before the Russians entered Mesa."

"Well, the Russians have destroyed New York City, and everything and everyone in it."

"My parents were heading to the Hampton's, but I am not sure if they made it out of New York in time," Ian said with concern.

Bill put his hand on Ian's shoulder, "Ian, because so many people waited until the last minute to leave, the traffic was backed up and they didn't make it out before the Russians arrived. Is it possible your parents got out, but…"

Frantic, "please, I need your phone," Ian asked in a panic.

Without delay, Beth grabbed the cordless phone and handed it to Ian. Ian called his mother's cell but there was no answer, so he called his father's, with the same effect, but he kept trying for the next few hours until what he presumed, the phone went dead.

Slumping in his chair, "it can't be. They cannot be dead."

Beth, who was standing next to Ian put her arms around him, "my dear, I am so sorry."

Ian turned his head to Beth's side and cried until he couldn't cry anymore, and when he was done, "I am sorry Beth."

"Honey, there is nothing to be sorry about. You are welcome to stay here as long as you wish."

"Thank you."

"Now, I will go make up the guest room and you can get some rest."

"Thank you," Ian said again.

"Think nothing of it," Beth said as she watched her husband.

"Go on, I will keep Ian company."

After a short time, Beth returned, "your room is ready. Come, I will show you where it is, and you can get some rest."

Ian, without a word, rose from his chair and followed Beth to his room, and once he was inside, he collapsed on the bed and cried himself to sleep. Now, he was truly alone, now that his whole family was truly dead."

For the next five years, Ian stayed at Smith Farm with Bill and Beth, and after they passed away from old age, Ian

43

took a horse from their stables after he released the other animals from their pins, then headed back to Mesa to see what happened after the battle between the Russians and the Americans. In those five years, communication with the outside world had been cut off, and Ian, Bill, and Beth had survived off what the farm had to offer, and lucky for them, there was enough food to get them through, but it was time to leave and see what happened in the world.

On horseback, it took Ian several hours to reach the outskirts of Mesa, and what he saw, was the destruction of everyone, and the closer he came to the city, it was no better off. For the people, well, the city seemed to be deserted. When Ian came by a grocery store, he found the doors were wide open, so he went inside, and the smell of spoiled food was overwhelming, but he resisted the urge to leave, as his hunger got the best of him.

Ian grabbed a cart and the first place he went was the isle that held the water and grabbed as many as he could carry. Ian then made his way through the other isles grabbing as many can and dried food as he could manage. Once he was done, he bagged everything up and tied them to the saddle of his horse, then made his way to Phoenix. Once he arrived on the outskirts – tired from his travels, Ian found an abandoned house near Camelback Mountain with a large backyard with plenty of grass for the horse to eat. Once the horse was eating and had plenty of water, he made his way into the house and made him something to eat after throwing out the spoiled food he found in the fridge. Once he had his fill, he found an empty room and went to sleep.

When Ian woke the following morning, he found he slept the night and most of the next day. "Wow, I must have been very tired to have slept until noon. I must see to the horse and make sure he is okay."

Ian got out of bed, washed his face, then brushed his teeth, and after he got dressed, he went to see to the horse. He filled the bucket he left last night for the horse with more water and watched as the horse drank greedily. "I am sorry boy. I didn't mean to leave you for so long. I had only intended to rest for a bit before making sure you had everything you needed," Ian said, looking over to a fishpond in the corner of the backyard, "well, at least you had enough water than what I left you last night, but it seems with you and the hot sun it's almost gone. Once you had enough water, I will prepare a place where you can rest out of the sun."

Once the horse was settled, Ian went back into the house and fixed himself a meal, and made some coffee, and after he had his fill, Ian went to scope out the neighborhood, to see if he could find a place that will be better equipped to keep a horse. When he came across a large house with a large backyard and plenty of grass for his horse to graze on, along with lots of shade from the trees, Ian went back to the house and packed and grabbed his things and once his horse was saddled, he went to what would be their new home.

"I think you will like it here. There is lots of grass to eat and water to drink, along with plenty of shade from the large overgrown trees to protect you from the sun. You should be very happy here," Ian said.

Once the horse was settled in the backyard, Ian went into the house and took a good look around. A family lived here, and he wondered what happened to them, but decided it was best not to think of it, so he went through and removed all the spoiled food and replaced it with what he grabbed from the store. He created a burn area in the backyard where he burned all the trash since there was no trash pickup. After, he took a nice long shower, and after, he turned on the TV to see if there was any news, but there was nothing but static, so he went to the master bedroom and lay down to go to sleep.

"Tomorrow is going to be a long day when I ride into downtown Phoenix to see what is there."

Ian was worried that he would find no one there since he hadn't come across a single soul on his long journey and prayed he would find someone in downtown Phoenix.

When Ian woke on the following morning, it was seven a.m., and after he had his breakfast, he dressed, then went out and saddle his horse and headed into town, and to his relief, he found people – several people there, and from these people, he learned that the governor called for all survivors to meet at Tempe Town Lake to discuss what was going to happen next.

After Ian arrived at the lake, he could not believe who he saw – *Trevor.* Ian quickly made his way to Trevor and when he was close enough, he called out, "Trevor!"

Trevor turned when he heard his name and he could not believe his eyes, "Ian! You are alive? I went looking for you and when I couldn't find you, I thought you were dead. What happened to you, man?"

"I headed out of town during the battle and found myself on a farm with an elderly couple who took me in, and after they died, I took a horse and headed here to see what happened to everyone. I was worried when I saw no one on my way into town and was relieved when I saw people as I approached downtown Phoenix, and then when I saw you…well, I am so glad to see you, Trevor."

"It was horrible. After the battle, there were so many people left dead, so I headed to Phoenix, where I've been ever since. Then when I heard that people were gathering to find out what the governor was going to do about the remaining people, I came here at once."

"Well, I am glad you are alive. Do you know what's happened with the rest of the world?"

"Yes, every state was hit by the Russians before they made their way back to their country, but before they could get there, they were attacked and destroyed by us and the English, then they destroyed all of Russia, but with the chemical warfare, many were left dead from all around the world. From what I heard, the world population is now in the thousands instead of the trillions it used to be," Trevor said shaking his head.

Ian was shocked, "chemical warfare? Are you serious? I had no idea," he said shaking his head, "this is crazy."

"Where have you been to not have heard about the chemical warfare?" Trevor asked.

"I was on a farm, far outside of mesa, where we had no access to TV. We did listen to the radio…well, after a time, we decided we didn't want to hear any more of what was happening. Maybe that was a bad idea, but it was nice to live without listening and worrying about what was happening. We just couldn't take it anymore. It was just too much man. Just too much," Ian said with shame.

Trevor placed his hand on Ian's shoulder, "I understand man," Trevor said, then they heard the crowd cheer, "here comes the governor. Let's get closer so we can hear what he has to say."

"Good afternoon, ladies and gentlemen. Our world is no longer what it once was. We have much to do to rebuild what we once had, but access to the resources we once had is scarce, as we do not have access to transport food and equipment. We must learn to do what we can with what we have available to us here. Farmers, we ask that you provide food to everyone and those who have skills that could help provide us with what we need. We are going to provide as many people as possible with electric cars and those who can ride a horse, we ask that you do. We ask those who have skills to build carriages and wagons, to place your name on the list here," the governor pointed to his secretary who was seated at a desk next to him. "We have been forced to revert to the days before we had technology. I am also going to continue allowing electricity to run free to all those who need it. If you find a house that has been abandoned, then you can claim it as yours. If you do this, you will need to notify my office of the house you choose so we can make a record of it. All other abandoned buildings will be broken down and what materials, equipment, and furnishing there are, will be placed in an area where everyone will have access to, along with all the furnishing and vehicles. I ask that those with a skill that can help us rebuild would be a great help during these times. Please, come and place your name and skill on this list," he said pointing to his secretary, "and where we can reach you. These are rough times, and we all must find a way to adapt," Governor Terrain said as he turned towards General Blye.

"This is General Blye, with what is left of the Army, this state is under martial law. They will continue searching for survivors and gather supplies to be distributed to everyone. Once a week we will meet here and provide what is needed. Keep in mind, there is not much, so please, take only what you need. In time, we will regain what we lost and adapt to this new world."

Everyone roared with acceptance and understanding and after Governor Terrain finished his speech, he ordered General Blye to distribute what they had and took down everyone's name and where they were living, and the skills they possessed that can help rebuild their city.

Once everyone was done, Ian informed the General of Smith's Farm, and what remained there, although he released the animals, he was sure they could easily be found.

Ten years later, as Ian was lying in bed unable to sleep thinking about those first few years after the Russians bombed Arizona, thinking of the last time he spoke to his parents, of course, he didn't know it would be the last time. Learning that his parents may have been killed on their way to the Hampton's because they waited until the last minute to leave New York, as traffic was backed up and they didn't make it out before the Russians arrived and bombed New York City bringing it to rubble.

Ian was safe where he was, but as the Russians were making their way through the United States, they were bombing all the cities they came across, as they were making their way to California, then back to their country. It was later learned that they didn't want to leave anyone alive to retaliate.

Once the Russians passed through Arizona on their way to California, then back to their home country, Ian knew, although he'd been gone a long time, he knew nothing would ever be the same again. When Ian tried calling his parents with no answer, and then later heard those who waited until the last minute, as his parents did, he learned they never made it out of New York City, because the Russians bombed the freeways killing everyone.

49

Ronny Whitman

After Ian returned to Phoenix, through Trevor, he learned when the Russians passed through California on their way back to Russia, the United States and England – of what was still left of the British Armed Forces, destroyed the Russian and Chinese fighters along with all of Russia and China, leaving only a desolate land. Then, when they learned that many were lost from the chemical bombs the Russians and Chinese dropped all over the world, it was a devastation like no other, leaving only a handful of people left that were spread out across the world with little to no communication. Everything they knew had changed. Their lifestyles had converted to what some call the dark ages. Oh yes, there was still modern technology, but that was reserved for emergencies, and it would be many years before that would change.

It was their regular meeting at Tempe Town Lake, where Governor Terrain would provide the people with updates and what the people needed – i.e. food and such.

"Ten damn years! Ten. It took us ten years before we finally felt safe to return to our lives. Or, at least what it is now. Safe to return to a somewhat normal life. Ten. I wonder what happened to Mark and his family. Did they survive? I tried calling his cell, but it was not working, as a lot of the cell towers were destroyed, so there is no way of knowing. I just hope they did," Ian said.

"Ian, it has taken ten years, but we are making it back. It may be slow, but it's happening. Maybe in another ten years, we will be even better off than we are now," said Trevor, his ex-roommate.

"Trevor, you might be right, but this is madness. I wish there was something I can do."

Ronny Whitman

"There is nothing you can do. All you can do is your part in helping get this city back to where it was. There are so few of us now, and the governor is right, we must work together to rebuild our city and country."

"Yes. Thank goodness some farmers survived and still have good farmland, if they didn't, we wouldn't have food."

"I agree, but even if there were no farmers, I am sure we would have found a way to grow food. For all of us to come together…with our help, we will continue to have food for everyone. Well, for as many as we can…we must. We don't know how many people there are outside of the city since we don't have a way to communicate," said Ian.

"Yes, but the Army has sent men across Arizona to find and locate any survivors and bring them to the city if they are willing, and any other farmers who can help grow vegetables and fruits, along with any cattle and other farm animals."

"Yes, we have reverted to using horses as they did in the old west so that we can get around."

"Well, we must do what we must to survive during these harsh times," said Trevor.

"You are right Trevor," Ian said looking at his watch. "It's time for the governor to make his announcement about the housing left abandoned."

"Then let us get there before it's too late."

Once Ian and Trevor made their way to the center of the park where everyone was gathered around the stage that was erected for Governor Terrain they stood waiting for the governor to arrive.

"Welcome everyone. As you know, in the beginning, we allowed you to choose a house that was abandoned and

51

requested you provide me with the address of the claimed property along with your name. Well, after time and with those homes that no one laid claim to, today we are permanently making those homes yours. Now, for those who had the original owner make claim, please present the new home you were allowed to choose, and we ask that you come up and form a single line and provide your name and address of your new home. Since there has been enough time for the original owners to lay claim, you will be given documentation of ownership for your house and the land it resides on. If your home is a farm and the previous owner has not laid claim to it, you will receive ownership, along with an agreement that you will provide food for everyone in the city. We are also asking those who can, to start opening grocery stores so the farmers have a place for people to obtain this food. Until we have a way to make money, we are asking those who open the grocery store to provide food, of only what is needed to the people for free."

There was a large roar of appraisal, but there was also concern among the people.

Governor Terrain raised his hand, "we do not have a way of making money, not with the way things are. Most banks are not in good operation since they were raided during the war. Besides, money is of no use to us right now. We must find a way to come together to help one another instead of working for profit. Yes, this is a barbaric way of living, but it is all we have for now. In time, I am sure we can return to a way of life we use to know, but for now, we must come together and help each other out without the need for money. Who knows, we may become a closer community and world as we never had before," Governor Terrain said.

The people roared with concern and rejected the idea, but Governor Terrain would not have it. "Stop! Look around," he said in a harsh yet firm voice. "We are not the world we once were before the war!" he yelled, then took a deep breath, and once he let it out, he continued in a calmer sympathetic voice, "we need to work together and share what we have with everyone. I am the elected Governor of this state, and as a former military general, it was agreed I would remain the leader in charge. When the time comes for our country and world to return to normal, then we will. This is not easy, but what good is money if there is nothing to spend it on? We must come together in a way to share what we have with everyone. Once our country and our world return to a place of normalcy, where we can use currency again, we will. We ask that we return to a place of trade, and for those with a useful skill, we ask that you place your name and skill on a list along with a way to reach you. Now, shall we begin?" he asked raising his eye, daring them to question his Authority, and when no one spoke, "well then, please form a line here," pointing to the place where a table was set up with a few military members to take down the peoples information.

Although there was some reluctance, the people could not argue with what the governor said, so everyone formed a line and provided their information.

"General Blye, how is martial law going?"

"Well, we have found those who were causing trouble and placed them where they would be given time to adjust to the way things are, if they don't, they will remain locked up in the base prison."

"Very well. I hope they will change their ways. I would not want anyone to be locked up in the world we are in now. We must find a way for all of us to come together so we can rebuild our world."

"Yes, I agree."

To everyone's surprise, everyone did come together – a community working together as one, including most of the criminals they had locked up. The governor continued martial law for another five years, and after a time, those who remained in jail were set free to live as the others but were warned if they broke the law again, they would spend their days in jail, and to General Blye and Governor Terrain's surprise, the people came together in a way they never expected – peace and harmony returned to the land, along with a way for people to start making money again.

Banks reopened, and currency was once again being used, even credit cards were being issued, but tighter than it once was, and knuckle-buster, a manual credit card imprinter, a device used before the electronic point-of-sale terminals were invented. Slowly but surely, life was starting to return to a sense of normal.

Chapter 3

Ian found himself happy in this new world. It actually surprised him to find he loved the simpler way of life. Yes, some things were beginning to return, but people were closer than they have ever been. He even heard from Mark and learned his family was alive and well, living high in the Flagstaff woods, in a cabin far from everyone. He learned that the city of Flagstaff, also came together to provide everything that was needed to keep the people alive and going.

Ian remained in the house and on the land he found, with the horse he took from the farm he lived on for five years. With what he learned from the Smiths, he offered his services to the farmers around him and found himself working on Smithy Farm helping with the cattle and horses. It wasn't the life he knew, but one he came to love. He felt at peace for the first time in his life and grew to come to terms with the loss of his parents. The people of this land were now his family.

When Ian was restless and unable to sleep, he found he liked to go for long evening walks thinking about what had happened and what his life once was, and where his life was going. However, something was knolling at him, a feeling that he was destined for something so much more, but what it was, he didn't know, and for some reason, walking made him feel close to the land, something else he didn't understand – why.

There weren't always dragons in the valley, but after the bombs fell during WWIII, it caused the protected shield that was created by Queen Allabella to collapse, and then

55

with time, as the earth loosened, it was enough to free Darca and her nest that was frozen for many millennia.

The first thing Darca heard when she woke was the roaring of the earth. The earth had always spoken to her as it did to Queen Allabella, and when her eyes snapped open, without hesitation, she burst through the earth and burrowed her way to freedom, free to fly the starry night sky once again. However, when she was high in the sky and looked down, it wasn't the land she knew, but a new and unfamiliar one that appeared to have been damaged by a great disaster.

Quickly, not knowing how the people of this land are, she cloaked herself so she could investigate this land without being seen, but it was late at night and there didn't seem to be anyone around, but she sensed this land was full of people she was unfamiliar with.

As Darca flew across the sky getting a feel for this new land, which was so different from the one she knew, as this land had tall buildings and – there, *what are those? I sense people in them.* What Darca was seeing were little boxes rolling across the land on what appeared to be hard ground with color lines. As she went to investigate, she spotted a human male – there was something about him that drew her attention away from the little boxes and people. This human male – for some reason, fascinated her, and she felt drawn to him, and the only time this has happened before, was when a human possessed magic. Intrigued, Darca moved closer to the man, wanting to get a better look at him, and when the man looked up at her, she roared and spewed fire, letting him know she was not one to be reckoned with.

Ronny Whitman

While Ian was taking his late-night walk, although it was a hot night, there was a nice breeze that made the heat tolerable, when suddenly he saw something from the corner of his eye, and when he looked, he saw something large fly across the sky. Ian stopped, so he could get a good look at what it was, but when he looked, there was something there, but he wasn't able to make out what it was. *It may be a night owl, although it seems quite large for an owl,* he thought. Shrugging his shoulders, he decided it was nothing interesting, so he turned his attention back to the path he was on, and just as he started to walk, he heard what sounded like large flapping wings – very large wings, and when he stopped to look again, he could not believe his eyes, it was a dragon. *No way! It cannot be a dragon!* Ian thought, shaking his head. He closed his eyes, and when he opened them again, yep, it was a dragon. A living breathing dragon, one of myths, was now hovering directly above him. *This is impossible.*

Ian could not believe what he was seeing – a dragon. A living breathing dragon, and when the dragon shot fire, he hit the ground so hard he was sure the gravel penetrated his shirt and embedded itself in his skin beneath. *What in God's name is happening? Where in the hell did this dragon come from, and why is it targeting me? Am I to be her midnight snack,* Ian wondered.

Darca, after giving the human her warning, saw the man drop to the ground. Sensing there was no threat, she decided to land directly in front of him, and for a long moment, she just stood observing the man, trying to get a sense if he was good or evil, and after a few moments, she smiled, he was a very good man, with a long-living soul, one that possessed great power, something he didn't seem

57

to be aware of, and so she decided, that this man was one she believed she could trust.

"Thy, human male, stand and look at me," she demanded.

When the dragon landed directly in front of Ian, he was sure he was going to be the dragon's dinner, but when she – yes she – he wasn't sure how he knew the dragon was a she, but he did, and when she spoke to him, he was shocked. *How can a dragon...animal speak to me,* he thought?

"Human male, rise and speak," the dragon demanded again.

Slowly and carefully, Ian rose off the ground, and when he did, he found himself standing directly in front of the dragon. He had to tilt his head back in order to see the dragon's face, and when he did, she was a formidable beast, one with spikes surrounding her head and two very sharp horns, but when he looked at her eyes, they were a type of blue he's never seen before, and they seem to sparkle with their own light. She was beautiful, Ian determined, but when he looked at her mouth, it was filled with very, very, sharp teeth, *ones I do not wish to meet any time soon,* he thought.

Ian took a deep breath and when he let it out, "you can talk. How is that possible?" he asked with amazement.

The dragon laughed, "silly human, do thy naught know all dragons can talk? How do thy not know this?"

Ian raised his eyebrows, "how would I know? You are the first dragon I have ever seen. You are...were believed to be a myth."

The dragon was shocked to hear this. *Myth, how can this be,* she thought. Then said aloud, "myth...how...can this be. There are...were many of my kind," she said, baffled by what Ian said, as she whispered, "myth's…how…how," as she looked directly at Ian, "can this be. There are…were many of my kind," she repeated.

"Maybe during the time you lived, but now they don't exist and were…you became to be known as myths," Ian said, feeling the need to explain what a myth was. "A tale that's been told, without proof they existed," he explained.

"Well human, as thy can see, I exist," she said with irritation, as she looked around her surroundings and then back to him. "What thee call thy self?

Ian smiled, "my name is Ian. What is yours?"

The dragon returned the smile, but bared her teeth and said, "thou will not be able to pronounce my name, but humans long ago gave me the name Darca, and thou may call me so."

Ian looked at the dragon's teeth, believing she was trying to intimidate him, but it didn't work, and he returned the smile, as he placed his hand on his chin, "Darca, that is a very fitting name for you."

"Thank thee. Ian, will thy help me learn the way of this new land and the people who reside on it?"

Ian smiled, "I would love to, but I don't think we should remain in the open. First, I think we need to start with your speech," he said with a smile.

"What do thy mean, my speech?" she asked with confusion.

"Well, it is old-world speech, not one of today."

Confused, so Darca reached into Ian's mind and looked through his memories and the way people spoke, and he was right, her speech would be strange to these people. After assimilating the information from Ian's mind, she gave it a try.

Ronny Whitman

"Good evening, Ian. I am Darca and new to this land. How was that?" she asked.

Ian raised his eyebrows, "well, that is very nice indeed. How did you adapt so quickly?"

"I read your mind," she said as if everyone can read minds.

Ian smiled, "well, that is a great ability," looking around, "I think we better go before we are seen. I don't know what people will do if they were to see you…a dragon. They could panic…fear what you may do to them and try to shoot you.

"Shoot me? How will they shoot me? Nothing can harm me," she said.

"Well, maybe during your time as weapons weren't as advanced as they are now. Now we have guns, explosives, and other deadly weapons that could possibly harm you."

Darca needed to understand more of the weapons Ian spoke of, so she reached into Ian's mind once again looking for these weapons, and what she found she did not like and was unsure if she would be safe from such weapons.

"These weapons of yours are very deadly. I am not sure if they will not harm me. I believe you are right. We must leave before we are seen."

From what Darca saw in Ian's mind, this time frightened her, and when she decided to look in Ian's mind again and saw these weapons he mentioned, she found what caused the destruction she saw from the sky – they were extremely powerful weapons.

Darca thought of where they could go, and there was only one place she believed would be the safest, but should she take him to her nest? Could she truly trust this human – Ian? Darca moved her head closer to Ian, so she could look directly into his eyes, which made Ian uncomfortable, but he did not move. As Darca looked into Ian's eyes, deep enough so she could penetrate deep into his soul, the way Queen Allabella taught her, and what she found, was enough to satisfy her decision, it was safe to take him to her nest.

Darca nodded her head, "we shall go to my nest where we will be safe."

Ian tensed, *her nest,* he thought. "Nest," he said slowly as he swallowed the lump in his throat. "How will I get there? And how will I know once I am there you won't eat me?"

Darca threw back her head and laughed, "Human, if I wanted to eat you, I would not take you back to my nest. I will fly us there."

"Oh, well that's good. On…you're…back," he asked cautiously.

"Yes, on my back, how else," she said with surprise to Ian's question, then without further words, Darca laid down and magically produced a saddle on her back.

Ian was shocked, "magic. You can do magic," he said with fascination.

"Yes. Now climb up my wing," she said as she stretched out her wing for Ian, "and onto my back. Once you are seated in the saddle, I will take to the sky, so make sure you hold on tight. Once I am off the ground I will dart towards the sky, and Ian, where I take you, you must tell no one, not ever, because if you do, I will be forced to destroy you." Although Darca said this, because of the agreement, she could never harm a human, but it was best not to tell Ian this – yet.

Ian took a moment to digest what Darca said, then nodded with understanding as he walked up Darca's wing and settled himself on the saddle she provided. Without further words, Darca stood and began flapping her wings until she was off the ground, although she planned on darting into the sky, for Ian, she decided to gradually make her way into the sky, and once she reached her desired height above the clouds, concealing them from being seen, she soared through the night sky towards her nest.

When Darca took off, Ian braced himself for a sharp incline, but he was wonderfully surprised when they rose into the sky gradually, and from what he could see from his position, Darca was a formidable dragon, one that could destroy anything that got in her way. She not only had spikes on her head, but he was also surprised, as he didn't notice this before, she had very sharp spikes all over her body.

You could not see them because I had them folded down so you would not be harmed when you climbed up my wing and onto my back, Darca said in Ian's mind.

"You read my mind again," Ian said with fascination.

Darca turned her head towards Ian, "yes of course," she said baring her teeth in a smile.

For the remaining time, Ian admired the land below and around them as they flew across the sky, not able to believe a forty-year-old man was flying on the back of a dragon, causing him to feel as giddy as a schoolboy.

Ronny Whitman

Chapter 4

Ian could not believe he was flying on the back of a dragon, an honest-to-god dragon, and when Darca started to descend, he realized where they were – directly over Camelback Mountain, and the reason it was called Camelback Mountain, was because some said the mountain looked like a camel, but at times if you look at it in a certain way, it looked like a dragon.

Well, I cannot say I am surprised, Ian thought.

This area was a beautiful place, that use to be surrounded by richly built homes, but now, now the land was as it was before people populated it. So, it was of no surprise that a dragon's nest – Darca was hidden there.

At the northeast corner, just at the top, was a large hole, where Ian believed Darca burst through when she awakened from her deep sleep.

Darca took a few moments to circle the area a few times to make sure there was no one around to see where her nest was, and once she was satisfied it was safe, she called back to Ian, "hold on. I must fold in my wings and fly straight down."

Without further words, trusting Ian to do what she said, once Darca reached the place she burst through, she folded in her wings and dived through the hole, and tunneled her way down until she reached her nest, and after sitting down, she stretched out her wing to allow Ian to climb down, then removed the saddle she produced for him. Once Ian was down, she turned in a circle and spewed fire to expand the area to a large open cavern, and once she was done, Darca turned her attention to Ian, taking from his mind, she produced a chair for him to sit on.

"Please sit, if you wish," said Darca.

When Darca drove into the hole, Ian closed his eyes as he held on for dear life, and once they landed and climbed off Darca, he saw the nest of six golden dragon eggs – *more dragons. Wow,* he thought with fascination. And when Darca used her fire to expand the cave to a large cavern and then provide him with a chair, he was once again astounded by her magic, but he was way too excited to sit down.

"This is amazing," Ian said, as he slowly turned to take in his new surroundings. "The eggs…your children? When will they be born?"

Darca turned to look at Ian, as she went to lay down on top of her eggs, with the need to protect them. It also helped to keep Ian from straining his neck from having to look up at her.

"My children will not be born for many years yet, which will allow me time to adapt to this new world and the people of this land. I also want to see if there are any other dragons still alive, that may have been buried…trapped as I was."

"Years? Wow! Well, it's probably for the best since this world will need time to get use to you. Do you truly believe there are more of your kind alive?" Ian asked.

"Yes, I do, and you can help me find them."

"What, me?" he asked with surprise. "How can I help?"

"You are not aware of this, but you have a gift, a power within you…magic."

"What! Me? I have magic? No, not possible," he said with shock and a bit of excitement.

"It is. I sensed it in you. It is what drew me to you. I sensed the power in you, although faint, it is there, and I can help you tap into that power."

"How? How can you help me tap into this power?" Ian asked with great interest.

Ian was astounded by the idea that he has powers. He remembered how he felt earlier, that something was different, *could this be it?* he thought.

Darca smiled and bared her teeth. "I can use my mind to enter yours and your soul, to that part that holds the memory of this power and bring it to the surface…return the memory of when you were a wizard.

Ian could not believe this. Shaking his head, *a wizard. What?* he thought, but the thought of having magic like Darca was thrilling.

"No, not just like mine, but you will have similar abilities," Darca said, showing Ian once again she could read his mind.

Ian smiled, "will I be able to read minds like you?" he asked smiling.

"Yes," Darca said baring her teeth.

Ian was not bothered by Darca showing her teeth anymore, he knew it was her way of smiling. "If you are to do this, how long will it take if I were to consent?" he asked.

"It will take only moments. We can begin now if you like?"

"No, not yet. I need time to understand this. I also need to acquaint you with this world."

"Very well, when you are ready let me know."

"Okay, great. Well, what do you want to do now?" Ian asked.

"Why don't you tell me about this new world and the people?" Darca asked.

"That could take all night. It's late and I haven't slept yet," Ian said looking at his watch, finding it was two in the morning.

Quickly, Darca produced a bed, an image she'd taken from Ian's mind. "Sleep then, and we can talk when you are well-rested. I will hunt for food while you sleep."

Ian panicked, "not humans!"

Darca laughed, "no, not humans. I will seek animals."

"What if someone sees you?"

"No one will see me, as I will make myself invisible."

Amazed, "wow, what a great power. Okay," he said climbing into bed. "I will sleep, and we will talk in the morning."

"Night human…Ian."

Darca flew across the night sky looking at the land and valley below, and how much it had changed from the time she remembered. It had buildings that looked to be made of metal and glass, and parts of the land were hard as stone. She also noticed a great deal of destruction, which appeared the humans were trying to repair.

Darca had to fly many miles east from where her nest was before she finally found what she was looking for – cattle. Without further thought, Darca flew down and snatched up four cows with her claws and quickly made her way to open land where there was no one to be found, and after landing, she became visible and released the cows from her grasp, then blew fire from her mouth cooking the cows. Dragons prefer their meat cooked, but if they had to, they would eat it raw.

After Darca had her fill, she made sure there was nothing left to show she was ever there, and when she was satisfied, she took to the sky and flew around the valley trying to learn as much as she could of this new world she found herself in. Once Darca was satisfied, she headed back to her lair and rested over her nest, laid down, and fell asleep just as the sun began to rise.

Ian woke from a well-rested sleep and when he opened his eyes, for just a moment, he had forgotten where he was. He quickly sat upright and moved his head back and forth looking at the cavern he found himself in, and when he rested his eyes on a sleeping dragon, he rubbed his eyes and looked again. Yep, it was a dragon, then it hit him, reminding him of the night before, no, it wasn't a dream.

"Good morning human…Ian. Did you sleep well?" Darca asked as she yawed, bearing her sharp teeth.

Ian was surprised last night actually happened. "You are real. I wasn't dreaming," he said with astonishment. Just then the cavern burst with light from the torches that lined the walls, giving Ian enough light to see his surroundings.

"No, Ian, you were not dreaming."

Ian slowly moved off the bed as he gave a big yawn, then took a good look around at the cavern before returning his gaze to Darca, and for a few moments, he stood there just watching her as if he was seeing Darca for the first time. Darca's scales were dark brown, no, they were a mixture of different shades of browns and blacks, with a hit of dark red and when the light hit it just right, a flash of orange and red, like the color of flames.

"It allows me to blend into the earth," Darca said.

"You read my mind," he said with amazement.

"Yes hum…Ian," she said with a smile.

"Wow! That's going to take a little getting used to. You are a beautiful dragon, to be able to camouflage yourself is

67

a great benefit, but to be able to make yourself invisible, that is amazing," he said.

"Yes, but there are times when it is easier to blend in with one's environment."

Ian nodded, "you are as big as a 747."

"What is a 7…4…7?" Darca asked, with confusion.

"It's a large airplane," Ian began to say when he saw the confusion on Darca's face, he went on to explain further, "it's a large metal plane that holds hundreds of people that can fly them anywhere around the world they want to go."

Darca raised her eyes, "does it have wings like mine?" she asked, stretching out her wings, which were as long and wide as a football field, possibly larger.

"No, well, yes. The plane has wings, but they cannot flap…move as yours can. They are stationary, which gives the plane balance to help keep them in the air."

"Oh, I see. Does it have a tail like mine?" she asked.

"No, nothing like yours. Yours is long with sharp spikes, that can knock down a building with one swipe," Ian said, moving closer wanting to get a better look. "Your whole body has sharp spikes with large ones across your back. Seeing them now, they are very deadly indeed," he said.

"Yes, they can be, but I keep them blended in my body and only show them if I am threatened," Darca said.

Ian smiled, "wow, that is amazing," he said as he continued to observe Darca, and, as if it was for the first time, he noticed her long mouth and sharp teeth. Her large almond shape brown…no, black…no, green eyes. *Weren't her eyes…when I first saw her, a rare type of blue…well, apparently her eyes can change color as well,* he thought. The top of her head has two large horns with small spikes

Ronny Whitman

in between them. There was no doubt, Darca was a beautiful and dangerous creature – dragon.

"Are all dragons like you?" Ian asked.

"No, I am an earth dragon. There are water dragons, that are blue and can live in the water. There are air dragons, which are white and can blend and move with the clouds. There are tree dragons, which are green and brown and live in the forest, and when needed, they can blend in with the trees. Those are only a few, but there are many more with many other colors."

"Wow! They must be beautiful, and these dragons, they may still be alive, but frozen…trapped as you were?" he asked with fascination.

"Yes, they can, and with your help, I can learn if they are still alive."

"Me? How can I do such a thing?"

"As I told you, the power is within you, and I can help you tap into that power. We can begin now if you like?"

Ian held up his hand, "no, not now. I am not ready for all that. What I am, I am starving. How do I get out of here so I can get some food?"

"I will create an entry for you, that will allow you to come and go. For now, if you like, I can provide you with food. What would you like?"

"With magic right?" he said with understanding. Ian looked up to the ceiling rubbing his chin, as he thought about what he wanted. "Hum, well, I'd like a big breakfast that includes bacon, eggs, hashbrowns, toast, waffles, and a large pot of coffee," Ian said, turning back to look at Darca, and seeing the confused look on her face. "Oh, right, you would have no idea what I am talking about. Can you take what I want from my mind?"

"Of course," she said, then looked into Ian's mind and created a small table and chair, then one by one she produced the food Ian wanted with his large pot of coffee.

Ian's eyes widen at the spread of food Darca magically created, and without delay, he sat down and dug into the feast before him, and once he had his fill, he sat back in the chair with his hands on his stomach.

"That was wonderful, thank you," Ian said. "How about you, are you hungry?"

"No, I had a large meal last evening."

"Well then, I'd like to go home so I can shower and change?" he said, and just like that, Ian was clean and wearing fresh clean clothes. "Okay, so you are not ready for me to leave," Ian said with a laugh.

"No, we have a great deal to talk about. I must understand this new world of yours."

"Alright, what would you like to know?"

"Tell me as much of the history of this world for the last several millennia?"

"Whoa, I cannot tell you everything, only as much as I can remember from history class. But I will tell you as much as I can."

Ian gave the history of the world as much as he remembered from class and books he's read. He wasn't much into history, so it was difficult, but it was enough to give Darca a good understanding of what happened to the world she remembered.

"But, for the current destruction you saw, well, there was a war between Russia and Ukraine. The Russian president was determined to own everything, and when he ventured outside his country to the countries that were part of the European Union after Ukraine joined the union, the United States and the United Kingdom, along with France,

Ronny Whitman

Germany, and other European countries joined together to stop the Russian president. In retaliation, he sent several bombs and dropped them all over the world. We were the least affected, although it doesn't show. Millions of people died and the whole world was left with a few thousand people left, maybe hundreds of thousands throughout the world. We are doing our best to rebuild, but it hasn't been easy."

"How horrible to have such weapons exist in this time."

"Yes, it is horrible. We have been forced…reverted back a few hundred years…in the way we travel. We used to travel by airplane, the ones I told you about, if we were going a great distance. Now, although we have cars, we are limited on gas, since we don't have access to oil as we use to. These restrictions force many people to stay where they are, and we walk when it's not too hot or some of us have started riding horses again. If we need to travel across the seas, although we still have planes, they are reserved for only emergencies. Instead, we've adapted the ships with sails, and we still can foretell the weather before sailing.

"Even though this happened, you are still further advanced than the time I am from. Tell me about the people who live here. How have they behaved…behaving after all of this? Are they angry and bitter?"

"To my surprise, after the initial shock, most of the people have come together. We are truly a nation…a world united. Many are working hard around the world to produce oil so we can have gas, along with the advantages we use to have, but I believe we are trying to make it better than what it once was. Gas is not ideal for our environment, but we are trying to get people to rebuild using natural energy. I believe we will be better and stronger than before."

Ronny Whitman

"I might, and if we can awaken the other dragons, we might be able to help you with transportation and many other things. This is something we can mention to your leader to establish a friendship between you and my kind. I can, with your help, open a doorway to other magical creatures who would be willing to help as well."

This fascinated Ian, *magical creatures?* he thought.

"Tell me, tell me of the time you came from?"

"My time. My time was many years ago when the land was open and full of trees and magical creatures…the fae and fairies were responsible for keeping the plants and the trees full and beautiful. Other dragons helped with the protection of the people and other creatures, and if needed, we offered transportation. The few humans that existed were called druids, who were also of magic, protector, and creator of the land. We all lived in harmony for many generations, but then something happened, a major catastrophe that locked me in the earth and asleep for all these years. I cannot tell you what that was, since I was asleep with my eggs. We do this until our children are ready to be born."

"Wow, it sounds like a wonderful life. Magic, how fascinating. To have humans and magical creatures living in harmony together is a wonderful dream. Magic, I would love to be able to do magic," Ian said without taking a breath with excitement at the possibility of being able to do magic.

Darca smiled, "well then, shall we begin?"

Chapter 5

"Begin? What do you mean? Wait, I need to use the facilities," Ian said.

Darca raised her eye, "facilities?" she asked.

Ian laughed, "I have to go to the bathroom."

Darca still did not understand what Ian meant and decided to read his mind instead, and what she saw caused her to burst out laughing. "You may choose a place in the cavern that will give you privacy."

Ian shook his head, but smiled at Darca, and without further words, he found a good spot and relieved himself, and when he returned, Darca noticed he wasn't as tense as he was before.

Sighing, "okay, I am ready. What do you have to do?" Ian asked.

Darca stood, which forced Ian to tilt his head back to keep eye contact with her.

When Darca saw Ian struggle to make eye contact with her, "there is no need to stand. It might be best if you lie down on the bed and close your eyes. Once you are comfortable, I will begin," she said, and Ian did as Darca asked, and once he was comfortable on his back, he closed his eyes.

When Darca saw Ian was ready, she pushed her mind into his and began with his current life and slowly moved backward until she found what she was looking for.

Ian was shocked by the strange sensation he felt when Darca entered his mind, and he was amazed at how he was able to see his life as she went backward in time. He saw his current life, then his teenage years, his childhood, his birth, and then she went to the life he lived before his current, where he was a cowboy in the old west. In another

73

life, he appeared to be a British soldier in the revolutionary war, and next, he was a woman – a mother of two children, but he couldn't tell what time it was before Darca reached her destination.

The landscape appeared to be a forest and there was an old man with long silver hair, along with a long silver beard and mustache. He was tall with a full figure, wearing a long gray robe that was tied at his waist with what appeared to be a rope. He was standing in what appeared to be a massive cave and nearby was a large black pot, Ian felt he was making some type of potion. How he knew this, he didn't know, when suddenly the old man stopped and looked up as if he was looking directly at him, but he knew this was impossible, then the old man spoke, "I have been expecting thee. All thee will need will be available to thee once thee return to thy time. I bid thee good luck."

With that, Ian was suddenly back in his time, and when he opened his eyes, he felt strange – different. Ian instinctually opened his hand, and in the center of his palm, he produced a small fireball, with that, all the information – the memories of the wizard flooded his mind. Ian was no longer Ian, the man of the twenty-first century, but a wise and powerful wizard from a time long gone.

Ian looked at Darca, and all the memories of dragons poured into his mind, "it is nice to see your kind again," he said and bowed in the ways of old, showing respect and honor to be in the presence of an ancient one.

Although Ian was himself, he was different and was taken aback by the way he spoke, his speech, and his behavior that was not his own. With this, Ian knew he was no longer the man he used to be, but a stronger and wiser one, with knowledge going back to the beginning of time.

This surprised Darca, "you know of my kind?" she asked.

"Oh yes, I have known a few of your kind during my life as a wizard, and as you know, I have lived a long time." Ian was surprised by his words, but knew what he said was true, and found he had memories that stemmed hundreds, even thousands of years, seeing his powers transfer from one life to another. *Fascinating,* he thought, then looked at Darca, "I am sorry about what happened."

"Happened? What do you mean by what happened? What do you know of my kind?" Darca asked, anxious to know what happened to the other dragons."

"Oh dear, I am sorry, but through the decades they were hunted and killed, and those that weren't, vanished to where I do not know, and during the rest of my…the previous wizard's time, I never saw them again. You are the first I've seen since the last millennia."

"They survived long past the time I lived, and if they vanished, then they must be asleep, and with your help, we can learn if they are still alive, and then I can send out the call to awaken them."

Placing his hand on Darca's leg, my dear…*my dear? This is not how I talk,* Ian thought, but waved it away and continued, "I will be more than happy to help. I hope they are still alive, it would be nice to see dragons in the world again."

"As do I," Darca said. "First, I need your help to acquaint myself with this time and these people. What do you think we should do first?"

"I think we should get a fill for what people would think if there were real dragons in the world. Can you still shift…*shift? Wow, the knowledge that's pouring into my mind is amazing…*into human form?"

"Yes, but it has been a long time. Do you think that is the best way?"

"Yes. Before you show your true self, you need to walk among the people to familiarize yourself with who they are now."

"Where shall we start?"

"This weekend is a celebration we call the new independence to celebrate our survival after the war. This will take place at a place called Tempe Town Lake. Your magic, can you still create illusions?"

"Yes."

"Wonderful. After we've walked among the people, we will test their reaction to the illusion of a dragon. After, we will decide what to do next."

"That sounds like a wonderful idea. What shall we do now?"

"Well, would you like to begin early? We can go for a walk in downtown Phoenix."

"That is a wonderful idea."

Without further thought, Darca made the change from dragon to a beautiful tall woman with long dark wavy hair and milk-white skin, and she was standing barefoot wearing a long golden robe. One's that was worn by the druids from her past.

Ian's mouth dropped open with shock, and after a few moments, he gathered himself and said, "wow, you are beautiful." When Darca smiled, Ian almost fell over. "You will drive the men crazy, but you might want to change from that," pointing at the robe, "to something more modern."

Darca looked down at herself dressed in the old druid robes, it was all she remembered of what people of her time wore.

When Ian saw Darca's confusion he said, "look in my mind and change into a pair of jeans and a t-shirt."

Darca did what Ian suggested and donned a pair of dark blue skinny jeans, a plain light blue crew neck t-shirt, and a pair of white tennis shoes.

Ian smiled, "wow, you are definitely going to get the attention from men and possibly women. I think it's best you remain by my side at all times."

Darca smiled and Ian almost fell over, as her smile only heightened her already existing beauty.

I better remember she is a dragon. A ferocious dragon, Ian thought.

Darca led Ian to a part of the cavern and blasted a hole through the mountain rock with her fire, and when Ian saw this, he was amazed to see fire coming out of Darca's human mouth, at the same time he was not. Once the entry was created, Ian followed Darca out of the cavern and into the bright afternoon sun, and when Darca turned, the entrance disappeared, cloaked by her magic.

"Ian, you must remember this entrance location. It will be the only way you can come and go," Darca said turning to look at Ian. "What?"

Ian was standing there with his mouth open, shocked at what he witnessed. "I know I have all the knowledge and wisdom of the wizard, but it still shocks me to see fire coming from a human mouth along with the magic you can do."

"You have the magic in you now. You can do almost everything I can."

Ian searched his new memories and found Darca was right, but there were many things he could not do, such as shapeshifting or being able to shoot fire from his mouth, but he did remember that he can create fire in the palm of his hands, so Ian opened his hand and a small fireball formed in the center of his palm. Ian smiled, he loved his new powers and looked forward to learning everything he could do with them.

"This is amazing. It's going to take a little getting used to," Ian said as a ball of fire floated over the palm of his hand.

Darca smiled, "so, where to?"

Ian returned his attention to where they were and pointed west. "We are going to have to walk, and at this time of day, it will be very hot, since it's a three-mile walk."

"Well, I can fly us there."

Ian shook his head, "no, that will draw too much attention."

"Remember, I can cloak myself."

"Yes, but I think it's best we walk like humans. It will help you learn our ways and the terrain. I will cool myself with magic from the knowledge I've obtained from the wizard."

"Ian, remember you are the wizard. He was you at a different time."

Ian smiled, "yes, you are right. Shall we begin?"

Darca nodded and off they went.

Ian was not surprised at the amount of attention Darca was receiving from the men and women as they walked downtown. To let everyone know she was not available, Ian placed Darca's arm in the crock of his.

"These buildings are very tall. I see there is much damage. If you like, I can repair them," Darca said, turning to look at Ian.

Ronny Whitman

Ian laughed, "yes, you could, but how will the people react to seeing a building instantly repaired? We don't want to do anything that could draw attention there is magic in the world. Not until it's safe."

"Of course, you are right. Turning to look at their surroundings, "this is an amazing place. Such a grand city with all these…what you called them, cars."

Ian smiled, "yes, it is grand, and yes, cars, but this is more than half of what used to be on the road, but what you see are electric cars." Seeing the confusion on Darca's face, "yes, I am sorry. They are…how do I explain this…you know lightening, how powerful it is?" Darca nodded in understanding. "Well, imagine that power captured and placed in the cars," looking at Darca, he still saw the confusion on her face. "Maybe you should just take what I am trying to say from my mind," he suggested.

Darca did and after she understood, "amazing, the way you have taken something so powerful and harnessed it to be used for what you call electricity and these," looking at the cars going by, "electric cars," she said with amazement. "This is a great power your people have."

"Yes, it is, and the person who invented electricity was a man who tied a key to a kite and flew it into the sky and when lightning struck the key, he felt the surge of electricity in his hand," Ian said, then turned back to the people around him. "What do you think of the people?" he asked, turning back to their original conversation. "What do you sense from them?"

Without telling Ian, Darca with a thought, repaired one of the taller buildings and the reaction of the people caught Ian's attention, and when he looked at Darca and she at him, she was smiling widely.

Ronny Whitman

"I could not help it. In doing this, it will help me gauge the minds of these people in the way they react."

Ian turned his attention away from Darca to observe the reaction of the people – there was no fear, instead, they were in awe at what they saw. *Maybe they will be accepting,* Ian thought.

"So, what are you getting from the people's minds?" Ian asked.

"They are not afraid but fascinated. They are wondering who could perform such a miracle. However, I am sensing some are uncomfortable and are worried about how or who could do this. However, I am not sensing anything that would cause me concern."

As Ian and Darca were talking, people began to swarm around the building, as did Ian and Darca, so they wouldn't be out of place and listen to the comments the people were making.

"Amazing," one woman said.

"How?" another asked.

"Why?"

"How is this possible and who can do such a thing," a man said in awe.

Everyone started looking around trying to find who or what was responsible, but they couldn't find anyone that stood out.

I think they will welcome my help, Darca said in Ian's mind.

Somewhat surprised, *yes, it is possible,* Ian thought.

Ian and Darca continued their tour through downtown Phoenix after the shock and excitement dwindled, and when Ian saw a burger place, one of very few remaining in operation, his stomach started to growl. It was early evening, and he hadn't eaten since breakfast.

"I'm starved. How about you, are you hungry…oh, maybe you prefer —"

Darca cut Ian off, laughing she said, "I can eat human food. I have been smelling it all day and I am eager to give it a try."

"Well, shall we go inside then?" he asked putting out his hand to her.

Darca took Ian's offered hand and together they went into the burger restaurant. It was a small restaurant with a few tables in the dining room, and behind the counter were a few workers. Ian was amazed. He hadn't come downtown in a long time, and to find such a place was amazing to him.

When Ian and Darca approached the counter, "how long has this place been here?" he asked.

The clerk behind the counter smiled and said, "it is my grandfather's place. It's been around since before the war, and after my grandfather passed away and after the war, my father wanted to bring something back to the people, so he reopened this restaurant, and we use the cattle from our farm," she said.

"That is amazing. I haven't had a good burger in a long time." Ian turned to Darca, "would you like to try a burger?"

When Darca entered the restaurant and smelled the food, she licked her lips in anticipation, and it took all of Darca's strength to keep from jumping over the counter and feasting on all the food.

"Ian sensed Darca's hunger, "choose whatever you like from the menu?" Ian said, smiling at Darca.

Darca licked her lips again and ordered two of everything on the menu, and the lady behind the counter eyes widened in shock, and looked at Ian wondering if this was a joke, but it wasn't a joke, and Ian shook his head no.

"Okay, two of everything," the clerk said.

Darca turned to Ian, "so, what are you having?"

Ian burst out laughing, which surprised the cashier, then ordered his meal and paid with the cash he had. There are still banks and people are still able to work and make money, but it's not like it used to be, cards are hardly used and cash is more the required form of payment, as it was before credit and debit cards were used. There is also trade, for people who don't have money, offering what they have, farming, and making quilts or knitting sweaters and socks, in exchange for something they need, and Ian noticed this restaurant also offers trade in return when he saw a customer offer several gallons of milk in exchange for a meal.

Ronny Whitman

Chapter 6

Ian and Darca went and sat down at a table at the back of the restaurant until their food was ready.

"So, this is the new world's way of feeding themselves?" Darca said.

"You mean restaurants? Yes, a lot of people eat out…well, use to eat out, especially when they are out and about, but many cook at home since there are only a few restaurants still open."

"Well, this is far advance from my time," Darca said a little too loud and the person at the table next to theirs heard.

Ian didn't miss a beat, and laughed, "your time. You mean before the way," he said aloud, but in his mind, *you must be careful with what you say aloud until it's time to reveal to the world who you are and the power you have.*

Darca laughed, "of course, what did you think I meant?" she said, and they both laughed, having the desired effect Ian wanted and the diner's return to their meals.

Just then, several workers began walking towards them with multiple trays full of food, which caught the eye of everyone in the restaurant.

"Where would you like these?" one of the workers asked.

Ian stood and pulled a couple of tables together and the workers sat the trays down. When Darca took two of the trays and sat them down in front of her, with Ian taking only one, he noticed the shocked looks on people's faces. "What, she's very hungry with a high metabolism," he said and smiled widely showing all his pearly white teeth.

After Darca and Ian finished their meal, they left the restaurant and began their way back to Darca's cave.

"Do you have to return to the cavern? I haven't been home since last night and I'd really like to shower and change clothes after being in this heat all day."

"No, my nest should be fine as it is well hidden. Is your home close by?"

"It's not far. It's very close to where you found me last night, but with this heat, I don't think we should walk, he said turning to Darca."

Taking the hint, without a word, Darca transformed from her human form into her dragon one.

Ian was shocked to see this and quickly looked to see if anyone noticed a big dragon sitting in the street on Central Avenue, and when he saw people still going about their business, he realized she was invisible.

"So are you," she said with a grin.

"What, me…invisible?"

"Yes. If you don't believe me, try to get that woman's attention who's coming directly at us."

Ian looked and saw the woman approaching and waved his hands to get her attention, but all she did was walk by without giving him any notice. However, Ian decided to stand directly in front of the woman and when he noticed she wasn't moving to go around him, he started to move out of her way —

"No, she will walk right through you."

Ian's head snapped to look at Darca, and she was right, the woman walked right through him as if he wasn't there, which caused a very strange sensation that made his whole body shiver.

"Climb up my wing. I have fashioned a saddle for you, then show me the direction to your home in your mind."

Ian did, and then they were off, an experience Ian found he could easily get used to, and when they arrived at his house, Darca, before landing in the backyard, used her magic to sit Ian on the ground as she shifted to her human form and only made them invisible once they were in the house.

"This is your home?" Darca asked with amazement. "It is nothing like what existed in my time."

Ian smiled, "yes, I am very happy with this home. I found it after the war and took it for myself. I was allowed to keep it later when our current governor allowed anyone to claim ownership if it was found no longer occupied by the original owner after a year had passed."

"Well, it is a fine home with fine furnishings."

"I am going to shower and change. Please make yourself at home," Ian said leaving Darca in the living room.

Once Ian was out of the room, Darca walked around the space looking at the pictures she believed were Ian's family, and the furnishings, how rich they looked and felt, and when she moved to the kitchen, it was very impressive. There was a large steel stove that had two doors in the front, with another large silver box with two side doors, and when Darca opened one of the doors, she was surprised at how cold it was inside, and there was food on the shelves. When Darca opened the other door, it felt much colder – freezing, and when she touched one of the packages sitting on one of the many shelves, it felt like ice. Darca returned and opened the first door again and felt an item, but it wasn't as cold as the other and she wondered why that was. *I will ask Ian when he returns.*

Just then, Ian came out from a back room and found Darca in the kitchen with a confused look on her face.

Darca smelled Ian when he entered the room, but it was different, and when she turned, he was entering the kitchen.

Ronny Whitman

"What is that I smell on you? It smells like the sea."

Ian laughed, "it's the soap I used to clean myself. What's wrong? You had a confused look on your face when I came in."

Darca turned back to the large box with two doors, "this box," pointing at it, "has two doors. One is cold but the other is like ice, why is that?"

Ian smiled, "that's called a refrigerator. The door on the left is the freezer and the door on the right is the fridge. The freezer is for items that need to be frozen if you are not going to eat them right away. The fridge is to keep things cold and from spoiling foods and drinks you use daily and don't require to be frozen.

"Oh," was all Darca said, but it was obvious she still didn't understand.

"Don't worry about it. In time you will come to understand and become used to it. What would you like to do now?" Ian asked.

"I think I should return to my nest, and we can talk more later."

"Okay. If you need me, call on me and I will be there. I'm going to take the information I received from the wizard and try to understand what I can do and how these powers I now possess work."

"A wonderful idea."

Ian went and opened the French doors they entered from, and Darca walked out and shifted as she did and flew off in the direction of her home.

Once Darca was in her cave, she laid over her nest with a pain in her heart – family. She missed her kind and her mate. *What happened to him? Is he alive and in a deep sleep like I was? Or,* she swallowed, *is he dead like so*

Ronny Whitman

many others, she thought. With sadness in her heart, Darca fell asleep and dreamed of her life before she'd awakened in this new world.

Darca was flying in the sky with her mate, "thee will never outfly me," she said.

"I can and I will outfly thee," said her mate, and without further words, Darca's mate took off with his wings tucked to his side and sped through the sky.

Darca, after getting over the shock of her mate doing such a thing, she too tucked in her wings and sped to catch up with her mate, and within a few moments, she was speeding past him and won the race.

Darca laughed, "thy can never be faster than me."

Tlachtga, her mate, raced over and snatched her up and joined their bodies together, and made love to her above the clouds. Later, Darca discovered she was pregnant and after she laid her eggs, she would sleep until their children were born.

"My love, I will miss thee."

"As I thee," Darca said. "We will be together in seventy-two moons and thee will have six new children to teach thou flying ways," she said with mockery.

"I will, and thou children will be better fliers than thy or me. What do thou think thy children will take after? Thee or me?"

"Thy matters naught, tis long as thy children are healthy."

"Well, then my love, rest, and I shall see thee in seventy-two moons."

With that, Darca watched as her mate flew away.

When Darca woke, there was a pang of great sadness in her heart. "It was the last time I saw him. I hope he still lives," she whispered with a sigh, and after a short time, she went back to sleep.

Ian and Darca were at Tempe Town Lake for the Independent festivities, and Darca hadn't seen so many people in one place before since her time and from the last few days.

"Where did all these people come from?"

"They came from all over the valley. What you see here is only a fraction of what we used to have, and I am sure not everyone is here. Plus, there are others spread across Arizona.

"Is this because of the war you mentioned?"

"Yes, but what we suffered is minor to what the rest of the world suffered. New York City no longer exists, as well as California and Washington, D.C. These are cities here in the United States, on this side of the world. Overseas, London no longer exists, as well as Paris, France, and other European countries. When there use to be trillions of people, there are now only hundreds of thousands spread across the world."

"How horrible. I am sorry to hear this. To see from my time, how the people I knew grew to be so many, to only be destroyed. What of the animals?"

"Ian smiled, *of course, she would be concerned for the animals,* he thought.

"Of course, I am," Darca said with a laugh.

Reminding Ian, that Darca could read his mind. "I'm sorry Darca. Yes, we lost many animals, but many have survived. There are probably more animals than humans now," Ian said with a smile.

This did make Darca smile, but Ian could see the sadness behind that smile. "Why are you so sad?"

Darca looked up at Ian, "I miss my kind…other dragons," she said closing her eyes as she lowered her head. "I miss my mate. The last time I saw him was after I laid my eggs and went into a deep sleep. I don't know if he is dead or asleep."

Ian took Darca's hand, "once we are done here, I promise I will help you find out. Now, I think it's time to see what these people will think if there were dragons in the world."

With Ian's newfound magic, Ian was able to project his voice loud enough to allow everyone around him to hear. "If dragons were real, would you want them in this world," Ian said as he singled for Darca to create her illusion of herself in the sky, "especially if they can help bring order to the world and return that which has been missing?" Ian yelled into the crowd of people who were going crazy over the illusion.

Everyone yelled, "hell yeah! That would be cool!"

"That would be wild man!"

"Yes-yes-yes! What a great idea if it were true!"

In front of everyone, Darca transformed into her true form, a living breathing dragon, and flew above the crowd of people as she breathed fire in the sky, then she did a series of somersaults showing her pleasure in the acceptance from the people.

The crowd went wild, but they didn't know if it was a real dragon or another illusion, so Darca landed hard on the ground causing the earth beneath her to shake which caused the people to go quiet.

"I am a dragon that has been asleep for many millennia, but now that I am awake, I want to help rebuild your land."

Ian looked around at the people, he could see they were shocked and unsure what to make of what they were seeing and hearing. *Darca, what are you sensing from these people? Are they scared or are they accepting?*

Right now, they are in shock, but I am not sensing any fear only confusion.

"Ladies and gentlemen, what you are seeing before you, is a real living dragon. She wants to help rebuild our world. She has great magic and is willing to use her magic to help."

Ian nodded at Darca, and it was time to show them what she could do. Darca turned towards the ruined building near the lake and just like that, it was like new again.

"It was you who repaired the building downtown." someone in the crowd said.

"Yes, it was me," Darca said.

The crowd went wild and cheered, and once the shock of seeing a living breathing dragon wore off, they roared with approval. After a few moments, Ian put his hand up and hollered for the people to be silent.

"Ladies and gentlemen, allow me to introduce you to Darca! She is here and wants to help rebuild our world! As you can see, it's within her power!"

Everyone surrounded Darca, fascinated by the large dragon. Although it bothered her to have so many people so close and touching her, she did not move. She wanted these people to trust her, to know she means no harm – suddenly there was a helicopter in the air hovering over the crowd. Darca turned to look at Ian, concerned about what this might mean.

Ian acted quickly, *cloak yourself now!* he said in Darca's mind.

Darca didn't hesitate and did as Ian said.

Go to the back of the crowd and change back to your human form, then uncloak and come back here.

In a few moments, Darca was by Ian's side in her human form as the military with guns drawn were rushing towards them.

What is it? Darca asked.

It's the military. I'm sorry, I forgot about them. They only appear in emergencies. For a short time, they were the law of the land. They know I'm involved, but not you. Don't say anything unless you need to, and if they do, I will help with what to say.

Darca was worried, she could sense these men were a threat, but she will do as Ian asked, not wanting any harm to come to these people.

Ian had to think quickly, of what he was going to say as the man in charge, a general, was heading towards him.

"You are responsible for this?" The general asked.

"Yes sir. How did you know? Your arrival was so quick."

"Well son, ever since the war, we've been closely monitoring the satellites. One of the controllers saw your little display, and when a real-life dragon appeared, he was shocked. After he recovered from his shock, he notified the officer in charge, and then I was ordered to assemble men to assess this dragon," he said pointing at the dragon.

He is a good man. A good soul. He wants to believe dragons are real, but the soldier in him needs to ensure there is no danger to the people, Darca said in Ian's mind.

"Sir, there is no danger. The dragon you saw wants to help us rebuild and bring peace to our world."

"How do we know this is the truth? We cannot take your word for it son. This dragon of yours disappeared as soon as we arrived."

"Wouldn't you if you saw a group of armed men? You descended on us with such force…a threat. To protect herself, she had to flee."

"Call her out. We want to speak with her to determine if she is a threat or not."

He is concerned that I am a new threat to this city and world, but his love for dragons…he wants to believe I am real. Tell him I will show myself and talk with him alone.

"She will agree to speak to you, but only you."

This surprised General Blye, and yet, he was intrigued. "Men, stand guard until I return. Where shall we go?" General Blye asked.

"There is no need," Ian said, and just then the general and Ian disappeared from the rest of the people.

The soldiers started to panic until they heard their general on their radios. "At ease men, I am safe. I have not moved, but merely become…invisible," he said to his men, then turned his attention to Ian. "Well son, where is this dragon?"

Darca decloaked directly in front of the general and greeted him as she bowed her head in respect, "have no fear general, I mean you no harm."

General Blye took a step back, "you…you…you are…" the general was stammering. He took a deep breath and gathered his strength and put on the face of a strong and powerful general. "What is your name and where have you been all this time, and why show yourself now?"

"My name is Darca."

General Blye could not believe his eyes – a real live breathing dragon was standing in front of him. *Wow, as a child I had always dreamed of meeting a dragon, and to see a real living dragon,* shaking his head, *this cannot be real.* But when he looked at Darca, he knew it was. Taking control of his excitement, "It's a pleasure to meet you Darca. I am General Blye of the United States Army."

"It is a pleasure general. I have been here for many millennia, in a deep sleep, frozen in time. I am here now because of your bombs. When your bombs fell, they caused the earth to shake, releasing me from my entrapment. When this happened, I woke from my sleep. I show myself now because I want to help the people of this new world and heal the land from the damage your bombs caused."

"How can you help?" General Blye asked with curiosity.

"I have many powers," turning towards the building she repaired earlier. "See that building over there, it was in utter destruction, and I repaired it. My strength and my ability to fly can assist you as well. There are many things I can do. There may be —"

Ian quickly cut Darca off. *Don't mention you can awaken other dragons, not until we've gained the general's trust.*

"a chance I can help restore your planet with food and plants."

General Blye rubbed the bottom of his chin contemplating what he was going to do with this information. He looked around at all the destruction that still exists at Tempe Town Lake, which is little compared to the rest of Arizona and the world.

"Darca, can you make this place and all that is around it like it once was before we developed this land."

Darca looked at Ian, and the general got the impression they were communicating, although he didn't know how.

"Yes, I can," Darca said, and without further words, Darca turned to the land, seeking the history of what the land looked like before humans built on it, and once she had the image, within moments Tempe Town Lake was as it was before man's creation.

General Blye turned slowly around admiring what Darca did. He could not believe it, the land appeared to be lush and full of plants, trees, and flowers he's never seen before. The lake, as it once was, was no longer one he recognized. It wasn't a man-made lake, but one of a natural creation. Looking out beyond where they were, he could see the confused and amazed look of the people and his soldiers outside the invisible shield, wondering what caused the transformation.

"Stand down men, this was Darca, the dragons doing," he said, turning back to Darca and Ian, "well, I'll be damned," he said and heard the people's ah's and oh's that were standing around them, reminding him they were not alone. "Ma'am, if you can do this, then our world has a chance to grow and strive once again."

"Yes general, but keep in mind, I will not do anything that will harm another human, animal, or plant. I am here to help, not destroy. Your soldiers," nodding her head at the men waiting outside their protective shield, "I will not allow them to harm anyone. Is that clear?" Darca said in a firm and Authoritative voice.

"Ma'am...Darca, we are soldiers, and we must maintain order here. There are those who don't respect the law and order we expect in this land."

"I understand general. You must do what you feel is right, but I will not be a part of that. I am here to bring balance and peace to this world, to ensure ALL life survives and thrives."

"Well, Darca, I will have to discuss this with the governing body of this land before I can commit. Will you allow me a day or so?"

"Very well general. What of your men?" Darca asked looking at the men on the other side.

"Before I receive the okay, I'm afraid I will have to leave a few of my men to ensure these people of this land are safe."

Darca reached for the man's mind to see if he spoke the truth, and she was pleased with what she found. He wants what she says to be true, to be a true partner with them and this world, and to help them rebuild and heal.

"I understand general. If you need me, blow this," just then, Darca magically produced a hollow plant stem. "When you blow into this, it produces a soft sound that I will be able to hear from any distance."

General Blye blew into the stem and was surprised at the sound. It was a soft hum that could barely be heard by human ears. "You can hear this sound, no matter the distance?" he asked with skepticism.

"Yes. It is not only the sound, but it also produces a vibration in the air and land…a type of communication that was used by the Druids in my time. Once I hear this, I will come to you here."

Druids? Druids of my time? I can scarcely believe it. Druids really existed. I must learn more, General Blye thought.

With that, the invisible barrier disappeared exposing them to the rest of the people who were waiting for their return.

"Stand down men," General Blye said, as he turned back to Darca. "Darca and I have come to an agreement. As of now, she is under my protection and is not to be touched without my direct order."

"But sir," one of his men started to say.

"Sargent, I have given an order!"

"Yes, general."

"Captain, leave ten of your men behind and the rest will return with me to base," General Blye ordered.

"You heard the general, move out!" yelled the captain.

Ronny Whitman

Chapter 7

"Well, where would you like to start first Darca?" Ian asked.

When General Blye reached out to Darca when he blew the whistle she gave him, it was only a few moments when he saw Darca and Ian flying towards him at what used to be Tempe Town Lake. When they landed, Ian was surprised to see Governor Joseph Terrain next to the general. At first, the Governor was shocked to see a dragon, but after talking with Darca and showing the governor what she could do, Governor Terrain accepted Darca as part of the protected animal population in Arizona.

"From what your Governor said, he seems to want to keep some of the buildings but not all of them," Darca said.

"That's because we don't have the people or the businesses to operate them as we used to before the war. I'd say we investigate all the larger buildings in downtown Phoenix to see which ones are still in operation and which ones are deserted and remove the ones that are deserted."

Ian and Darca walked Central Avenue in downtown Phoenix and removed more than half of the buildings, replacing them with open land filled with lush's trees, cacti, and rare flowers Ian's never seen in Arizona before.

"These flowers you've been creating, where are they from?" Ian asked.

Surprised by Ian's question, "from the land, where else?" she said as if confused by the question.

"But these are plants and flowers I've never seen before."

"The land speaks to me, and with the information I receive, I create what you see here."

"That is amazing! I hope that is something I can do."

Ronny Whitman

"You can in time," Darca said, baring her teeth in a smile.

For the next several months, Ian and Darca went around Arizona fixing buildings and homes that were destroyed and clearing the destruction and replacing it with new life.

"We have done such a great job with Arizona, and I think it's time we travel to the other states and across the world," Ian said.

"Ian, I cannot do this alone. I think it's time we check if there are other dragon's still alive in the world. If so, they can help, and this will go a great deal faster."

"Oh yes, I am sorry, I had forgotten. That is a wonderful idea. When do you want to do this?"

"Tonight is a full moon, so when the moon is high in the sky, it will be a perfect time, because it's when the power of the moon is at its strongest."

"Great. How about I go home and get some rest and meet you later. Where do you want to do this?"

"Yes, I will as well. At my nest. You remember where the entrance I created for you is?"

"Midnight. I will be there, and yes, I do."

When Ian arrived at Darca's cave and entered through the secret passage she created for him, he was surprised to see a large fire with a hole in the top of the cavern for ventilation.

"The fire, as you know with your wizard powers, this element is the strongest to use when summoning."

Since Ian became a wizard and learned about his powers, he couldn't help but still think like a regular human. *It's going to take a while to get used to,* he thought.

"And you will, come and stand by the fire on the opposite side of me."

"Okay." Once Ian was on the opposite side of Darca, "what do we do next?" he asked.

"Put your hands out to the fire and focus all your energy on the fire while you use your senses to reach across the land to locate any dragons that are still alive but in a deep sleep. At first, it will be light, like a small ripple in the air. With this, you should be able to sense if they are still alive. Once you sense them and touch them with your energy, without knowing it, they will feel your presence…your power. Once you have hold of their energy, I will then reach into your mind, and through your mind, I will enter theirs and help them wake from their deep sleep."

Ian did as Darca said and after a short time of concentration, he was surprised at how easy it was for his mind and spirit to leave his body in search of the power and energy of other dragons that may still be alive, and for Darca, he prays there was, especially her mate.

When Ian tapped into a dragon, he was surprised to find it wasn't far from where they were. The dragon was in Sedona, Arizona, and once he reached that first dragon, it was as if that dragon's energy merged with his and Darca's, and with all three of their energies, Ian began to sense others – hundreds of others, possibly thousands, as they flooded his senses. At first, he didn't know what to do, but then he stopped, and once he found the dragon's location, his spirit flew to where it was, and once his mind connected with the dragons, along with Darca's, it immediately sent a signal to all the dragons around the world at the same time. A powerful and amazing experience, Ian was proud to be a part of.

Once Ian connected with all the dragons around the world, Darca immediately sent out the call for the dragons to wake, and as they began to wake, she sent her location, and bid them to come to where she was. She provided them with as much information about the new world as she could before she broke the connection, but before she did, she tried to find the thread that linked her to her mate, but there was no sign of him, which saddened her, but she refused to give up hope he still lived.

"It is done," Darca said.

"Wow, that was amazing. The way I felt being outside my body, then to feel you enter my mind, using my energy – power to send the call to the others was…I don't have the right words."

"I felt there are many dragons still alive."

"How long will it take before we know?"

"It's hard to say. It took your bombs and fifteen of your years before I woke, so it's hard to say."

"Will you know when they rise?"

"Yes, I believe so, and you will know if they are nearby."

"There is still much I need to learn about my powers."

"It will come in time."

It was twenty-four hours later when Ian felt – sensed the first dragon awake, and it was very close. He believed it was the dragon he felt in Sedona, so he immediately reached for Darca's mind, *I sense a dragon in or near Sedona.*

Darca, without asking, quickly, but gently, entered Ian's mind and with her and Ian's powers, together they reached for the dragon that Ian sensed, and when she reached the dragon, she communicated to it who she was and when and where she was from, and where she is now. *Can you come here?"* Darca asked.

Ronny Whitman

The dragon responded, *yes, show me your location and I will come now,* he said, and Darca did as he asked, and the dragon, who was another earth dragon burst through the rock formation that surrounded him – that concealed him for centuries. When he burst through the rocks and dirt, he cloaked himself as he did so, and headed to Phoenix. *I am on my way.*

A thousand years ago, Drago, was named by a powerful and wise druid. His true name, no human would be able to pronounce. As Drago flew across the sky he couldn't believe after all these centuries an ancient one still lived. When he went to sleep it was during the time humans were hunting dragons after one of their own betrayed them by providing information on how to destroy them. They all believed it was safe to go into hiding and sleep until it was safe to return. *How many years have I been asleep?* he wondered.

As Drago was flying south across the land, he was amazed by how much the world had changed. There were many buildings he was unfamiliar with, and there was some type of hard ground with little boxes that could go very fast but was pleased to see there was still a great deal of open land until he reached the Phoenix city edge, where he found even more buildings, longer and taller than he has ever seen. The closer he came to downtown Phoenix, he could see Darca's work. Only a dragon could heal the land like this, along with the fae and fairies.

All dragons had the ability to sense when another was close, so she knew when Drago was near and sent him an image and directions to where he could find her, at Tempe Town Lake.

When Drago set down directly in front of Darca, he bowed his head in respect, "good day Darca, a human name," he said with a smile. "I too was given a human name, Drago."

Darca bowed her head, it filled her heart to see another dragon. "I am pleased to see another dragon, It has been many years since I saw another one of my kind. I sense you are a young dragon."

"Yes, I was born only a couple thousand years ago. My Lady, I sense thee are an ancient one. One who's lived longer than any I have known."

"Ancient one?" Ian asked, forgetting he had the knowledge already in his mind.

"Yes, those who have lived longer than another are called ancient ones, but I am hoping there are others like me, even older than me, that are still alive," Darca explained, then turned her attention back to Drago. "Yes, I lived in a time when the druids were powerful and worked with the fae and the fairy people, along with the dragons. We lived together open and free."

"I heard of those times, I have only been around for two thousand years before I went to sleep when there were many humans, but most of the magic people had left or gone into hiding. What of the other dragons?" Drago asked.

"It saddens me to see the magic people are no longer here, but," looking at Ian, "with Ian's help, we can return them to this land."

Drago turned to Ian, "you are a wizard then?" Drago asked, already sensing the power within Ian.

"Yes, I am," Ian answered.

"For the other dragons, you are the first to answer the call," Darca said.

"Before I went to sleep, there were hundreds if not thousands of dragons still alive, but with the humans hunting us," turning to Ian, "with the help of wizards, we decided to go into hiding, and then to sleep."

Darca was shocked at what she heard and turned to Ian. *This is a surprise. In my time wizards and druids would never betray a dragon,* she said to Ian.

The way Drago was looking at Ian made him uncomfortable as if he could be Drago's first meal after wakening. It caused him to take a step back, ready to escape if need be.

You have nothing to worry about with me around. He will not harm you.

Are you sure about that? He's looking at me as if I am going to be his first meal after wakening.

He will not harm you. I will not allow it.

Alright, I trust you.

"How can this be? Wizards, who use to be druids, were loyal to dragons. They would give their life to protect a dragon."

"Through the years, wizards were turned…persuaded by humans that dragons were evil, that we only saw humans as food," Drago said, then turned to Ian with hate in his eyes.

"To hear this saddens me," Darca said, turning to Ian, *this is why he looks at you as a threat.* "Ian is not a threat. He has been a great help to me, by helping me adapt to this new world. I helped him come into his powers, powers he wasn't even aware of."

Ian seeing Dargo's hesitation, "Drago —"

"Only those I trust call me Drago," he said with a snap of his teeth.

Drago was a large dragon, bigger than Darca, with very sharp spikes, from the top of his head down to his tail with a large double sword-like tail. His eyes are black as coal and his feet and arms were deadly. He was not a dragon to be reckoned with.

"Forgive me, I meant no disrespect. If you can look into my mind like Darca can, then I invite you to do so, so you can see I am someone you can trust."

Drago stared at Ian for a long time, giving him the stare of death, but after a few moments he turned to Darca, "if you trust him, then I shall trust him as well."

When Drago looked at Ian with eyes that promised death if he betrayed him, Ian was relieved and pleased when Drago told Darca he trusted him, and once he heard this, he let out a breath he didn't know he was holding, which caused Darca and Drago to look at him.

"What, you scared the shit out of me with those eyes that promised death by way of your next meal."

Drago burst out laughing, he actually laughed. Ian had no idea dragons laughed, since he hasn't seen Darca laugh, but then —

"Do not think I have not thought about it. I have not eaten in many years," he said with a snap of his teeth.

"Stop teasing the man Drago, he knows we do not eat humans."

"He made a joke, an actual joke," Ian said astonished by Drago's reaction.

"Maybe thee do naught," he turned to Ian and snapped his teeth again.

"Stop Drago, dragons swore long ago to never eat or betray humans."

"That was before humans started betraying us," Drago said with anger.

He will never forget those days humans started hunting his kind, but this was a new world and if Darca, an ancient one believed in these humans, then he will give them a chance.

"You did not eat humans, did you?" Darca asked.

Drago, for a long moment, stared at Darca, but then said, "no, no matter what happened, I did naught betray the agreement between dragons and humans, but Darca, there were those who did to defend themselves."

"I am relieved to hear this and sadden by what our kind had to endure. I will not hold it against them if they will again honor our agreement," Darca said. "We must…this is a whole new world. These humans need us. We have a chance to renew our relationship with the humans and return the magical people to this new world, to live in harmony as we were always meant to."

"I have heard the stories of the way we use the live, to be able to do so again, and in this new world…to be able to experience such a place pleases me a great deal. Darca, there are many dragons that will awaken who feel as I do, but together, I believe we can convince them to return to the old ways, and I am sure there are dragons that are still alive from thy time."

To hear this gave Darca hope that her mate might still be alive. "Do you know for sure, that there are dragons from my time?"

"Before I went into a deep sleep, yes, there were a few still alive."

"Then with the two of us…if there are any other ancients still alive, together we will convince them to return to the old ways. I have given these humans my word of trust and protection."

Ian had been quietly listening to Darca and Drago, and at first, he was concerned at what Drago was saying, but then he reached into his mind, the memories of the wizard, and found what he was looking for, dragons living in harmony with humans, then one wizard who turned to the dark side spread rumors that there were rogue dragons going across the land hunting humans for food, and in the process destroying many villages. It was not the dragons, but the Anglo-Saxons who were killing and destroying the villages because the people would not bend to their law.

Humans were deceived by this bad wizard and could not be at fault for what they did to protect themselves. It was the wizard who was loyal to the dragons that convinced them to go into hiding, to sleep until the world was in a place where the humans will accept them once again."

"May I interject," Ian said, "the wizard is where my powers come from, he knows...knew what happened. There was a wizard who went to the dark side and spread the word, the destruction was created by the dragons when in actuality, it was the Anglo-Saxons. This evil wizard, who called himself Dornazi, convinced people the dragons had turned against the humans and were hunting them for food and destroying the villages. It was this wizard who warned the dragons and asked them to go into hiding...into hibernation...deep sleep. And," turning to look directly at Darca, "the fae queen, Darca, your mate, I believe he went with her when she left this world.

When Darca heard this, she began to hope once again that she will see her mate one day. "Ian, are you sure?"

"Darca, I cannot be sure, as my memories of that time are still sketchy, but if what I just saw is true, then yes."

"Oh Ian, I hope you are right."

Drago knew of the wizard Ian mentioned, as he worked closely with this wizard. "I know the wizard thy speak of, and he was a good and honorable wizard. We did what he asked, and now, what he hoped may finally be here."

"Drago, Ian is the wizard reborn. I helped him gain his powers and when he traveled to the wizard's time, the wizard was expecting him. I believe he knew this was the time you were waiting for."

Drago looked at Ian and watched him for a few moments, then decided to ask, "may I enter thy mind to see thy truth?"

"I offered before, and the offer still stands. Yes, you may enter my mind."

Drago didn't hesitate, he quickly entered Ian's mind and shifted through his memories until he found what he was looking for. There, standing by his caldron was the wizard he remembered, but older than he knew. He watched as Ian's spirit arrived and heard what the wizard said, Ian is who the wizard used to be. After Ian left the wizard's cave, the wizard turned to Drago, *you can trust him. He is me reborn.* This shocked Drago, he had no idea the wizard would be aware of his presence while he watched Ian's memories. He had forgotten how powerful the wizard was. *Thank thee, old friend.*

"Thou is the wizard. Forgive me for doubting thee old one," Drago said as he bowed his head to Ian.

"There is no need, I understand your reason for being cautious."

"We will wait for the other dragons to rise, and once we are together, we will help Ian open the doorway to the Fairy Realm."

In the next few weeks more and more dragons rose all over the world, and Darca, as the only living ancient, was respected and looked to as the leader, so when she asked

107

them to come to Phoenix so she could explain what happened since they went into hibernation, they did as she asked without question.

When Ian heard that hundreds of dragons had awakened and were coming to Phoenix, he thought it was best they met the dragons outside of the city and from human eyes. Ian believed if the people saw this many dragons, they would become fearful, not to mention how they were going to feed all of them.

When all the dragons gathered in an open field ten miles outside of the city limits, Darca was surprised to find among the first group of dragons to arrive, were three other ancients that lived during her time – Toldore, a blue water dragon, Rango, a red fire dragon, and Ki, a white energy dragon, three that had been around as long as their old leader Beladore.

When Darca saw the ancients, she bowed her head, "it is an honor to see thee still alive and well."

"And thee, my dear," all three said at once. "We believed thee were lost when thy wizard Merlin, Queen Allabella, and us dragons failed to waken thee from thy deep sleep."

Surprised to hear this, "I wondered why I had not woken before now," she said.

"When the great fire fell from the sky, ye were protected…a shield created by Queen Allabella and Beladore, but when they went to waken thee, thee would not waken. Many thousand years passed when they tried again, but because Beladore was stricken with grief after having destroyed a dragon —"

"What, Beladore had to destroy one of us?"

"Tis so. Darca, he had no choice, Cillian was very evil and learned dark magic from the wizard Dornazi. Beladore tried to reason with Cillian, to no avail, and was left with the only option he had, to destroy Cillian. It took Beladore, Tlachtga, Queen Allabella, and Merlin to destroy Cillian. It broke Beladore, and he went to sleep, and without his powers, Queen Allabella, Merlin, Tlachtga, and the rest of the dragons, could not wake thee."

This surprised Darca, "my mate must have been grief-stricken believing I and our children were lost to him forever."

"Yes, tis true. He wanted to go to sleep until you wakened, but Queen Allabella convinced him to return with her to the Fairy Realm, along with any other dragons. He accepted this, and when you woke, he was to return, but I am afraid the Fairy Realm can only be opened by a powerful wizard."

Darca was struck with great pain when she heard what happened to her mate, but then hope rose again when she learned where he was and that a powerful wizard can return him. "Toldore," turning to Ian, "I believe this is the wizard thee speak of reborn. Ian, do you have the memory of how to open the door to the Fairy Realm?"

Ian was listening intently to Darca's and Toldore's conversation, and when he heard that the wizard he use to be had the power to open the door to the Fairy Realm, he searched his memories on how this was done, but he could not find the answer, and he didn't understand why, if he had all the powers of the wizard they spoke of.

"Darca, I am sorry, but I do not. As you were speaking, I searched for that information, but I could not find it. Is it possible it was a different wizard?" Then Ian was hit with the possibility of – "Merlin? You said his name was Merlin?" Ian asked with excitement.

"Yes, Toldore said Merlin. Why, does this name mean something to you Ian?" asked Darca, then turned to Toldore, "is this possible?"

Toldore looked at Ian, "if tis was Merlin, thee would have his powers. Tis possible, thee are naught ready yet, tis why thee have no memory," said Toldore.

"Merlin? Could it be the Merlin that was from King Arthur's time? I cannot believe I am that wizard. However, I am still learning what my powers are, so I may not be ready yet," Ian said, turning to Darca with sadness, "I am sorry Darca. Maybe one day I will have the power to return your mate to this world."

"King Arthur. I have heard of this Arthur who lived during my time, but he was a young prince and naught a king yet," said Drago.

"It's alright Ian. I know you will when you remember. It may not be until you come fully into your powers. I and my children were lucky to be spared from such a fate long ago, and we survived all these years, a few more will not hurt," she said.

"Toldore, tell me what happened after I went to sleep…with our people and why Queen Allabella left this world for another?" Darca asked.

"My dear, as thy wish," Toldore said, then went on to tell Darca what happened after she went to sleep, about the great fire that fell from the sky, everything up to when all the dragons decided to save themselves by going to sleep until the time it was safe for them to rise again.

"Meters," Ian said, regarding Darca and Toldore's conversation regarding the great disaster. Seeing their confused looks, "sorry, regarding the rocks that fell, they come from space, outside of the planet, debris from other planets that were destroyed. Throughout time, these have

Ronny Whitman

been responsible for the destruction of our Earth…planet many times, destroying life that no longer exists today, as well as the ice age."

Toldore listened carefully to the way Ian talked and began to adapt to the new English tongue. "Ian is right, there were many times when these great rocks fell from the sky and destroyed a great deal of the land. As the human race grew, although many continued our friendship, an evil fae, one you and Queen Allabella missed, began to turn the people against her and the fairies. Although Queen Allabella was able to stop him and his followers, she thought it would be best and safer for the humans if they left this realm, so Queen Allabella created a new realm she called the Fairy Realm that could only be opened by a great and powerful wizard, who would be born from the most powerful druid priestess, but he would not be born into this world for many generations."

"To hear this saddens me. Queen Allabella was a great fae, one I was pleased to call a friend. I hope one day I will see her again."

"My Lady, I am sure thee will."

For the next several days, more and more dragons awakened and were given instructions to go to Phoenix, and every day, more and more were arriving from all over the world and were taught the way of the new world and given a choice to recommit to the agreement between human, dragon, and fairies.

Within six months, Darca learned there were thousands of dragons still alive, and knowing her mate was no longer of this world, she believed he was safe in the Fairy Realm, and she was sure one day he would return to her. Instead of focusing on her mate, she decided to turn her attention to

Ronny Whitman

her eggs since they will be hatching sooner than she thought when she first awakened. She's already been preparing them for this new world, as well as teaching them the ancient ways through their mental connection.

After meeting with all the dragons, Darca was pleased they were willing to return to the old ways and the code of honor. It was time to send the dragons to where they were needed the most. Darca asked Ian to speak to his governor to see where they could be of use, and where they would be accepted by the humans that populate this world.

"Governor Tierran sent word to all the leaders across the states and the world, and he was pleased with the response he received. Of course, after their initial shock, when they learned dragons were real and alive," Ian said with a chuckle.

"We are ready to go where we are needed, we only need to know when and where," said Tal, another ancient that recently arrived.

"He's waiting to hear how the people will respond to the knowledge that dragons exist and are alive in our world. He doesn't want people to fear a dragon when they first see them…you."

"When will you know? The dragons are getting impatient. Although they fed well before making the journey here and can go a long time without food, they will need to feed soon," said Darca.

"We should learn how we are going to feed the dragons tomorrow," Ian said.

"Very well. I am tired, so I am going to retire for the evening. Do you need a ride home?" Darca asked.

Ian smiled, "no, I am learning how to use my powers, so I am going to teleport myself home," he said with a grin.

"I bid you good night then."

"Good night."

Darca jumped into the air and started for home with sadness in her heart. Although she has accepted she may not see her mate for a long time, in seeing all the dragons, she carried a heavy heart. When Darca arrived at her nest, she took a few moments to check her eggs before settling down over them, and once settled, she sighed, she missed her mate very much, and after a few moments, she was asleep.

Chapter 8

Once they received word the dragons would be accepted, the dragons were sent out across the states and the world to help where they were needed. If any humans were aggressive – a threat to a dragon, Darca was to be notified at once. A law was put into place, that it was against the law for any humans to harm a dragon, and if a human was to break the law, Darca and Ian would go and educate the humans and give them a chance to resume their lives in tandem with the dragons, letting them know they were there to help humans not harm them. If the first would fail, they would be jailed, and a third offense would be life in prison. This, Darca did not want. Every human and animal deserves to be free to live in the world.

However, with the power the dragons possessed, they could control any situation, but unlike before, they were ordered, that no matter the circumstances, they were to control their anger and honor the agreement between dragons and humans, as the humans were ordered to honor their agreement as well. With the help of the dragons, the world began to return to a life before the war, but better than ever before, a world that it should have been all along.

It was fall, and soon it would be winter solstice, and Darca felt it was time to return the fae and fairies to this new world, and hope for her mate as well.

"It is time to return the fae and fairies to this world. They have the power to heal this planet, returning it to the life it was before man destroyed it, by removing what humans did, in the toxic chemicals they used. Everything henceforth will be organic, creating a pure and clean planet, including your vehicles," Darca said.

Ronny Whitman

"The fae? You said I can help return them, but that information still has not come to me. How am I to do this?" Ian asked.

"Tonight, I want you to search your mind for the memory that holds that information. Once you have it, search for those who also have this gift, present, future, and past. It doesn't matter as time does not exist, and once you connect with those who have the power, you will create a circle of protection. You will also need to seek the crystal that will guide you to the door that will grant you entrance to the Fairy Realm."

"I can do all of that?" Ian asked with astonishment.

"Yes, and much more. Go, and return to me in a fourth night to share with me what you learned."

"Very well. Good night, Darca," Ian said as he turned to leave, then stopped. "Darca when will your children be born?"

"Soon Ian, very soon. Now go, I must rest."

Ian turned and left, but he heard the sadness in Darca's voice and wondered about the cause, but he will have to inquire about this on a different day.

"Your majesty, how may I be of service?" Darca asked Queen Allabella.

Queen Allabella said, "Darca, thank ye for coming. I request yer assistance to fly me across the land to visit the fae that lives several moons away from here."

Bowing her head, "of course, your majesty, but thy has the power to teleport. Why do thee require my assistance, if thy do not mind me asking?"

"Ye are right Darca, I can, but if I do, my power will be sensed, and I do no want them to know I am coming."

Ronny Whitman

"I understand and will do as thy ask. Is there reason to be concerned?"

"There is. I have been hearing that some of the faes are using their power to harm humans and that cannot be allowed to continue if true. With yer help, with yer cloaking ability, I can see for myself what is happening."

"Then I am at thy service. When will thee like to leave?"

"On the morrow at first light."

Darca woke. It had been a long time since she thought of Queen Allabella, and found she looked forward to seeing her again.

After Ian returned home, he went to the backyard where he created a circle with tiki torches, lit them, then sat Indian style in the center of the circle. He took a white and purple candle, along with some incense, and once they were lit, he closed his eyes and allowed his mind to calm, and after a few moments, his soul rose and traveled back in time, in search of what he needed that would allow him to open the doorway to the Fairy Realm.

After a short time, Ian began to hear words in his mind, *tatu mawa chetu maeta pata may yu.* Then, he heard, *these are the words you need to open the door you seek. Form a circle of protection with other druids, with an inner and outer circle. While you are standing in the center, you will draw a star on your right hand,* the voice said, and then Ian was given the image of a pentagram to place on his left hand, and on his right hand he was shown an infinity that was crisscrossed to form eight points with a circle in the center as he heard these words, *slice your left hand to spill your blood on the ground,* then he was shown a staff with a diamond type crystal on top, Ian believed was the crystal he

116

was looking for, and once this was done, he felt them, the ones who were to help him, as he heard these words: *when you are ready, you only need to call on us and we will be there. We are your protectors.*

Ian returned to the present with the information he needed and how to find the crystal he needed to perform the ritual. It was in Ireland. Although, he feels this is not how the wizard before him opened the door. His power was so great he didn't require such a ritual. "Maybe in time I too will have that power. Ireland? I need to go to Ireland. I will ask Drago if he knows of the place I need to go."

Ian reached that place in his mind that held the information that revealed more of his powers and spent the night learning all he needed to know for what he was about to do. In doing so, he was becoming a true wizard, and one day soon, he will have all the powers he once had all those years ago. "And maybe one day," he said with a grin, "I will grow a long white beard," then he laughed.

Darca met with Drago and the other dragons wanting to make sure they were doing well and not causing any problems with the humans.

"Is there enough food for everyone?" Darca asked.

"There is. Since Ian used his power to triple the cattle and sheep, there's been enough food for all of us."

"Have you heard from the dragons overseas?"

"Yes, they check in regularly. They are doing well. The humans have accepted them and treat them like family."

"I am pleased to hear this. Ian is preparing to perform the ritual to open the doorway to the Fairy Realm."

"This is wonderful news. Let us hope when Ian opens the door, the dragon's on the other side will return.."

117

Hope flared again in Darca, as she thought, *maybe my mate will also return.* "How many dragons do you think escaped into the Fairy Realm?" she asked.

"It is hard to say. Once we speak to the queen, we will learn this information," Drago said.

"Were you there when the dragons went to the Fairy Realm?" Darca asked.

"Yes. Queen Allabella said when it was time for the dragons to return, so will she. With what you said of this Ian, who was the wizard I knew, if she knew this day was coming —"

"It is possible. She has the ability to see into the future."

"Then now may be that time."

Darca and Drago went to the other dragons that remained in Phoenix and discussed their idea with them, and they too were pleased and excited that they may see their brethren again.

Clear across the world in what was left of the United Kingdom, in particular, Scotland, on the Isle of Skye, which was saved from the destruction that the rest of the United Kingdom suffered. Some believe it was due to the fae, that they had formed some type of protection around the island, but no one was sure.

The dragons that decided to return to Scotland have been working hard to repair the land to what it once was when they lived free, and it was becoming a magnificent and magical place, one only knew through myth and legend.

The forests were full and vibrant as they once were, with flowers and trees no one had ever seen, if not for centuries. Homes and castles that were once in ruin, were restored to their former glory, and the Scottish once again had their clans and wore the traditional tartan as their ancestors did centuries ago. The people return Scotland to the place it was before the English claimed it as their own, and the rest of Scotland was doing the same, returning to the way and beauty it was always meant to be.

Ireland and England were also returning to the way things were, and something happened, something no one believed was possible or real. The true wizard, that myth and legend believed was Merlin, had awakened from his deep sleep when Terra spoke to him, telling him it was time to wake and return the rightful king to his throne.

When Merlin woke after centuries of being asleep in the cave, the one he created that concealed and protected them all these centuries.

"It is time my king, for thee to awaken and resume thy rightful place as king of Albion," he said and clapped his hands, which created a loud boom and after a few moments the horses and men began to wake from their deep sleep."

"Merlin, where are we?" one man asked.

"Bruce, thee are in the cave I brought thee. Do thy naught recall?" Merlin asked.

Bruce shook the sleep from him and took a good look around, yes, he did remember this place. It was the place Merlin insisted they come and wait until they were needed again. "Merlin, our king, where is Arthur?"

Merlin smiled, "ah, tis there he lies," Merlin pointed at the figure lying covered in the center of the circle of men, and once all of Arthur's men were awake, did Merlin give the command to awaken Arthur. "Rise King Arthur, thee are needed once again."

With that, Arthur woke and rose to his feet. "Merlin, what year is this?" he asked, yawning.

Merlin smiled, "ah, My Lord, tis the year of our lord 2022."

Arthur spun around so fast to face Merlin he nearly lost his balance. "2022, so long," he said.

"Yes, My Lord. The world has no king and requires one that will bring balance and peace to the world. Magic has begun to return, and man, woman, and creature live in peace once again. I also sense an old friend from long ago, has been reborn and is the one responsible for this peace."

"If man and woman live in peace, why am I needed? This friend, do I know of him?" Arthur asked.

"Although they live in peace, they still need a ruler. Do thou recall I told thee that one day thee will be needed when the world needed a leader most? Nay, tis naught a wizard thee know."

Arthur put his hand to his chin thinking, trying to recall what Merlin told him all those years ago. "Yes, when the world has no leader and was in dire strait, thus when I will rise to bring order and balance once again. But thee said the world lives in peace."

Merlin smiled, "yes, My Lord, thus is the day. This world was almost destroyed by a great war and many of its people perished, leaving little around the world. This is another wizard I mentioned, he is one that's been reborn, and the man he is now, is just coming into his powers and he too has the ability to return the fae and fairies to this world. He has already awakened the dragons from a deep sleep."

This concerned Arthur and he put his hand on the hilt of his sword as if ready to pull it from its sheath. "Dragons? Thou telling me dragons survived?" Arthur asked, turning to his men, "men prepare thy selves for battle."

Merlin smiled, "nay Arthur. They are not the dragon thee knew. Dragons have never been our enemy. Tis was one dragon that was our enemy, and he no longer lives. These dragons have returned to the old ways, to the agreement made by the dragons and Fae Queen to live in peace with humans. These dragons live among us in peace and harmony."

Arthur relaxed the hold of his sword, "thy speak the truth?"

"Yes Arthur, I do."

Suddenly Arthur's stomach growled as did the other men, and with a wave of Merlin's hand, a large round table appeared filled with food and drink. "Eat and drink, then after, I will call the dragons here and thee will see for thy self. Once word spreads that the rightful king has returned to Albion, we will find thy castle and remove the protection spell I placed on it to hide its location, preserving it until it was time for thee to return to its throne. Thou will not only be king of Albion but king of the whole world of Terra."

When the men saw the food, they wasted no time in digging in, as did Arthur and Merlin, and once they had their fill, Merlin sent word to the dragons to come to where they are. The dragons were shocked to learn there was another wizard alive in this new world and immediately sent word to Darca, who relayed this information to Ian and the other dragons around the world.

It was evening when Darca and Ian were standing outside the base of Darca's cave when Darca informed him of the news about Merlin.

"Are you kidding me! Another wizard and you say the other wizard that woke is the one named Merlin, the one you believed me to be? If so, then who am I? Wait, the

Merlin, who was the wizard to King Arthur, and you say King Arthur is alive and well?" Ian was shocked. Another myth and legend were alive in this new world.

Darca smiled, "yes Ian, he is alive. We did believe you were the wizard Merlin, but this proves it is not true. I am sure this Merlin will know who you were, which we will ask when we meet him. All of us dragons were surprised to hear this. As you know, Drago knew of him as the great protector of all dragons, and Arthur was only a boy before he became this great and noble king, one he was pleased to learn is still alive in this new world. Merlin intends to return him to the throne of Albion and become the leader of the rest of the world."

"Wow," shaking his head, "King Arthur and Merlin…oh, the round table…King Arthurs Knights, they too are alive?" Ian asked with excitement. He grew up on the stories of King Arthur and his knights of the round table, and to know he is real and alive in his time was the most amazing thing besides learning he was a wizard and dragons were alive.

Darca laughed, "yes Ian, they are all alive. Merlin is requesting all the dragon leaders around the world and you Ian, the other wizard to go to Albion and meet the new king and become part of his coronation as the only and true king of Albion and the world, and we are to give our allegiance to this new king.

"Wow, I cannot believe King Arthur and his knights, along with Merlin are alive. Yes, oh yes, we shall go. I cannot wait to meet the most famous king of all time…King Arthur."

"Yes. I have already sent word we will attend."

"When will this be?" Ian asked.

"In three moons…months," Darca said.

"Wonderful. I will continue to work on getting the information we need to return the fae and fairies to our realm."

"Yes, and I am sure Merlin can help since he is the one with the power to open the door."

It's been three weeks since Ian gathered the information he needed to perform the ritual and went to inform Darca and Drago of want he needed to do and he did it without the help of Merlin, which made Ian smile. *I am definitely coming into my powers. Soon, I will be as powerful as Merlin,* he thought with a chuckle.

At dusk, once Ian reached the lake, in what used to be Tempe Town Lake, which was now called Dragon's Valley, he informed Darca and Drago what he learned. "I need to go to Ireland," Ian said. "Drago, can you reach into my mind to see the place I was shown, and see if you recognize it? Also, I received a message from Merlin. He said I am his old friend, who he remembered as Cardiff. When he knew him, he was a young wizard just coming into his powers, so he was pleased to hear his old friend has been reborn and looked forward to meeting me. He asked if I would allow him to read my soul. I of course said yes."

Without further to-do, Drago went into Ian's mind and found what Ian saw, and immediately he knew where the place was. "It is west of Dublin. There is a small stone circle where the old druid's rituals would be held. I can fly you there if you are willing?" Drago said baring his teeth. "Did Merlin say he would join us in Ireland?"

Ian laughed, although Drago came across as a scary dragon, one not to be reckoned with, Ian also noticed he had a sense of humor. "Ireland is a long way for me to ride on your back," Ian said with concern. "Unfortunately,

Merlin will not be able to attend. He is busy preparing Arthur for his coronation, but he believes with the help of the other druid's I will be able to open the door to the Fairy Realm."

"You have nothing to worry about. I can make it very comfortable for you, and we will arrive within a day. That is unfortunate, I would like to have seen him again."

"You will when we attend Arthur's coronation. How fast can you fly?" Ian asked, wanting to know how it was possible they could arrive in just a day.

"Yes, that is true. I can fly as fast, if not faster, than what you call a plane."

Ian raised his eyebrows in shock. "How will I be able to hold on if you are going that fast? Not to mention breathe."

"Do not worry Ian. We have the ability to shield you from the force of the wind. It will be like those planes of yours," Darca said.

"Really?" Ian asked with amazement.

Drago smiled, "yes. We can leave at sunrise if you like?"

"Yes, that will work for me."

"Very well. Be ready to leave in the morning. I will arrive at your home, and we will leave from there."

Ian, without delay, returned home to prepare for tomorrow's flight. He gathered warm clothes and what he needed to perform the ritual.

The following morning, just as the sun began to rise, Drago arrived at Ian's house, and just like Darca, he formed a saddle on his back and extended his wing to allow Ian to climb up. Once Ian was situated on Drago's back, Ian felt the air shift, then disappeared altogether. When Ian reached out his hand, he felt an energy that surrounded him, *a*

shield. Amazing. When Drago took to the air, Ian felt nothing and was able to breathe easily, and when he became hungry, he used his own magic to produce food for himself. *I love having powers,* he thought with a smile.

Drago laughed, *powers, powers have been a part of my kind forever. It is nothing to be fascinated about, but a part of our everyday life.*

For you maybe, but for me, it is all so new, and I am loving having these abilities. Maybe in time, I will also feel as you do.

Yes, I am sure, possibly after you lived a thousand years.

Ian laughed, *I am human, I will not live a thousand years. I will be lucky if I live to be a hundred.*

Remember Ian, you are a wizard now, and the wizards I knew lived for over a thousand years.

To hear this shocked Ian, *a thousand, I could literally live a thousand…maybe more years. What would I do with myself to live all those years and see people I know die.*

At first, it will be difficult, but in time you will become accustomed to it. Yes, you will love friends and loved ones, but you will have new friends and people who you will call family.

Yes, you might be right.

I am right. I am a dragon who has lived a couple of thousand years, and in this time, I have seen much.

Well, I will have to take your word for it, Ian said, and for the rest of the flight, Drago and Ian flew in silence while Ian contemplated on what Drago told him.

When Drago and Ian arrived in Ireland at the stone circle, Ian immediately recognized the place and was pulled in the direction to the right where there was a large mound.

125

"There," pointing at the mound, "we must go there." Without delay, Ian went to the mound and Drago followed behind, and once Ian was on top of the mound, he felt a strong energy coming from beneath. "Here, we must dig here," Ian said.

Drago raised his brow, "dig? Why not use your power to raise the crystal to the surface."

"Oh, yes, you are right," Ian said, turning to Drago, "one day I will get use to these abilities," he said shrugging his shoulders.

With that, Ian reached into his mind and found the spell he needed, and when he uttered the words, the ground rumbled and shook before it lifted in the air, and there, several feet down were the staff and crystal he was looking for. It was nothing special, but a simple stick and crystal, but when the crystal came close, Ian could feel the power it held, and with his mind, Ian beckoned for the staff to rise and come to him, and it did as he bid, and once it was in his hand, he replaced the soil and turned to Drago. "I have what I need. Let us return to the stone circle and call for the others to join us."

With the staff and crystal in hand and the words filling his mind, Ian sent out the call to the druids from past, and present, to reach for a dragon in their time to bring them to Ireland or if they had the power to teleport, to come to Ireland when the moon was high in the sky in two days hence from this night.

In two days when the moon was high in the sky, and while Ian was standing in the center of the stone circle, people – druids began to approach, appearing out of nowhere, with some in physical form and others in spirit, and together

Ronny Whitman

they formed the first inner circle and then the second, an outer circle.

"Hello, and welcome," Ian called out.

Everyone called out, "hello," in return. "We received your call and are here to help you open the door to the Fairy Realm," one said.

Ian smiled, "yes, I am pleased to see you, do you know what needs to be done? Oh, I am Ian."

"Yes. I am Joel, tis a pleasure to meet ye. Do ye have the staff and crystal?" the man with what sounded to be an Irish accent asked.

Joel was the leader of a group of druids that were from England, a group who knew this day would come, but they didn't know who would be the one to hold the power that would open the doorway to the Fairy Realm.

"Yes, we," turning to Drago, "located the day we arrived and summoned you."

Joel nodded, and once the circle was complete, Ian instructed the druids to stretch their arms out to their sides until their fingers were almost touching. With Ian standing in the center, and his mind holding the staff, Ian produced a dagger from thin air, and after taking it in hand, he took a deep breath, as the others began to chant om, he sliced his left palm, then closed his hand into a tight fist to squeeze out the blood until it fell on the ground. Ian stretched out his arms with his left palm up and the staff in his right hand, he began to chant, "tese maete pata naete," as he placed his left palm on top of the crystal and allowed the blood to drip down, then put out his arms to his side and said these words, "tato maca chenu mate pata maete," looking at the oak tree that sat a few feet away, and repeated the words over and over, and after a few minutes had passed, Ian saw a shimmer on the oak tree, and shortly after, a crack formed in the body of the tree with light spilling out.

When he saw this, he called out to the others, "focus your energy on the fairies who are of pure heart and soul and ask them to enter our realm to help heal our planet. Do not allow any fae with evil intent to come through."

When the door fully opened, the first two faes that came through were male, which Ian felt were scouts to ensure it was safe to enter. Once the two males turned and gave a nod, two female fae came through, followed by, what Ian believed was the fae queen. She was richly dressed and bore the demeanor of one of royal blood. Searching his memories to find when the wizard before him laid eyes on the fae queen, he found he was correct, she was indeed the fae queen. Following behind the queen were dozens of fairies of all sizes, and after the last was through, Ian felt it was time to close the door.

"Hello, tis nice to see ye again," said the queen.

Ian bowed, "Your Majesty, it is my pleasure. I was not expecting you to appear," he said.

"How could I no return to this world after all these centuries. Ye have a question for me?" she asked.

Ian smiled, "the dragons have returned. Are there other dragons living in your realm?"

The queen smiled, "aye, and when I return to my realm and share what I have learned here, I am sure some, if no all will want to return."

"This is wonderful. As I am sure you know, this world is very different than the world you remember."

"Aye, tis so, but tis no lost. Ye are here and the fae has returned," the queen said, turning towards the fae who have spread out and begun healing the earth. "As ye can see, they are already working at healing the land."

Ian turned to the fae and the little fairies, and indeed they were healing the earth. There were flowers where there were none and the trees seemed younger and more lushes than when he first arrived. It was beautiful.

"There is also a different feeling in the air…peace," Ian said.

"Aye, tis so. I must return. If ye need me, ye only have to reach out to me using yer powers and ye no have to be here. Ye can create these stone circles at any place ye wish. All ye need to do is bless them with the energy ye hold," she said, then placed her hand on Ian's head and a burst of light flowed from her hand to his head. "Now ye have the power ye need to call on me or visit my realm if ye choose to."

The power that entered Ian's mind, filled him with information on how to contact the fae queen and enter her realm. "Yes, Your Majesty, I have the information and I will if you are needed. If you wish to return, you only have to call on me. But Your Majesty, Darca lives and she hoped to see you again. Also, she was hoping her mate was with you in your realm."

"I will. Darca, ah tis good to know my old friend has awakened. Tell Darca, one day I will return and see my old friend again, but for now, to protect this world from the evil fae, I must return. For Darca's mate, tis true he is in my realm, but do no tell Darca yet. I must return, so I bid ye good day."

Ian was disappointed, but understood what the fae queen meant, and was sorry he could not bring Darca's mate with him when he returns. "I understand and will honor your request," Ian said, then opened the door just a crack, enough for the queen to slip through, returning to her realm.

Ronny Whitman

Chapter 9

After Ian and Drago returned to Arizona, he was astonished at the sight that lay before him. It was no longer the place he left – a desert. It was now a lushous and flourished land with a variety of flowers he didn't recognize.

The fairies have been hard at work while I was gone, he thought.

Ian didn't realize the fairies had already made it to the states, and at first, he wondered how, but then the knowledge flooded his mind, they have the power to move in the blink of an eye. Some birds and insects that were flying around were unknown to him and the lushes trees, bushes, and flowers were also unknown to him. In a place that was once a vast desert, was now a beautiful paradise with the cleanest air he's ever breathed.

I never thought in a million years I would see dragons and fairies existing, working side by side with humans, Ian thought.

"You won't live a million years. Maybe a thousand," Darca said with mockery.

"Reading my thoughts again," Ian said with laughter.

"We are connected, but if you wish, I will not —"

"No, it's fine. It will take a bit of getting used to is all."

"I never believed in all my days from before and now to see such a sight," Darca said.

"With what it was before the war, I feel the war was to our benefit. Without the war you would not be here, nor," turning to the sight before him, "these dragons, fairies, animals, flowers, trees, along with the ponds and lakes, it's a scene out of a fairytale."

"I too am amazed, but this was how it was…how it should be. If you listen, you will hear the earth singing with joy, and the people around the world are living in harmony. This was the world I lived in, and now it is yours."

"Is there a way to make it better?" Ian asked.

"Yes, we need to rid the earth of everything toxin, which includes a lot of technology you have now. Can these people do that?"

"I believe they can if you explain to them the benefits of doing so, and how we can provide them with alternatives."

"I believe that can be done, now that magic has returned to the world, so has the ability to travel."

"Then let us send a message to all the leaders around the world to come here to Phoenix, by traveling in the way of the dragons and/or magic, or with the assistance of fairies. To do this, we will prove there are other better and cleaner ways to travel."

"Agreed. I have sent word to the dragons, and they will relay my message to the leaders they protect."

Within a week, all the leaders from around the world arrived in Phoenix and were now standing in the place at Tempe Town Lake where the buildings and stadium us to be, but now covered with green grass, trees, flowers, and plants of some that were known and others that were unknown, to hear what the wizard and the ancient dragon Darca had to say.

Ian and Darca took the place at the head of the gathered crowd, "hello and welcome to Phoenix. We gather here today," turning to Darca who was standing to his left, "so we may speak to you about the changes we need to make to protect this planet and the people who remain. As you all know, you were brought here by dragons or by fairy magic. This was done to show you a different way of travel, versus using automobiles or aircraft, which is part of the changes we need to make," Ian said, then he turned to Darca to continue.

"The planet is being healed by the fairy folk, and to ensure she remains healthy, changes must be made. Things need to be removed and replaced with that which will not harm our planet. Would this be something you would wish to see?" Darca asked.

A roar erupted with the crowd in acceptance of what she was saying.

"If this is what you wish, we will remove all the chemicals, that includes your gasoline that man has created, along with any toxins that harm our earth."

"If you remove gas, how will people travel?" a man asked.

"How did you come here today?" Darca asked.

"We came by dragon," some yelled, while others yelled, "we came by fairy magic."

"And how long did it take you?"

One said, "by dragon…a day."

Another said, "by fairy magic, it was instantaneous."

"Then why can this not replace your aircraft? Your cars? Did you not use to travel by horse? We must change the way you use technology, in order to protect our planet. With what I have brought here, dragon magic and fairy magic, this can easily be accomplished," Darca said.

"For one or a few is simple, but if there were to be hundreds that want to travel together, it will be difficult," someone said.

"But not impossible. Magic will help to power your aircraft to carry a large number of people. It can be done. Do you not agree?" Darca asked.

"Yes, we so do," they all said.

Ronny Whitman

"Then, return to your homes and the dragons and fairies will rid your lands of everything that will harm our planet, and then they will work with you to create what will work."

With that, everyone left by magic or by dragon.

"Wizard, open the doorway." said the fairy queen.

Without question, Ian opened the doorway and what he saw come through, he couldn't believe – dragons, lots and lots of dragons, and once they were through, he closed the door as he heard, *do not tell Darca, there is a surprise for her.* Ian smiled knowing what he believed that surprise could be.

Darca woke with the feeling of movement under her, and when she lifted herself off her nest, she saw her eggs begin to hatch. *I did not expect them to hatch yet, but maybe the time we were frozen gave them the time to mature,* she thought as the first baby dragon broke through its egg, a male, then the second, another male, next, a female, then a male, and then two more females. Darca was so pleased and yet sadden that her mate was not around to see their children.

Ian, I am a mother. My eggs hatched and I have three girls and three boys. You must come to see them soon. For now, they must feed.

Congratulations Darca! I look forward to meeting your children when it's time.

Thank you, Ian.

Several weeks after Darca's eggs hatched, Ian arrived at the cave to meet her children. "They are wonderful," Ian said with amazement.

133

"They are the first dragons to be born in many millennia."

"Then, there must be a huge celebration."

"Yes, we must call all the dragons and fairies, along with any who wish to see my children."

"Yes, I agree. Let us set the day to be the first day of Samhain when the moon is high."

"Yes, that would be the perfect time."

And so, the first dragons birth announcement was created, and an invitation was sent to all around the world to come to Phoenix and meet the first dragons to be born in the new world – millennia.

A few days after Darca's children hatched, Ian received the invitation to attend King Arthur's coronation that will take place in two days.

"Ian, you must go. He is an old friend and I know he wishes to see you again. I cannot go, and I have already sent my refusal and the reason why. Merlin is pleased to hear there are new dragons born in this new world."

"You will be very much missed," Ian said. "But I am looking forward to seeing the famous Merlin and King Arthur and his knights."

Darca laughed, "Ian, you sound like a child."

"I am. This is the most amazing thing to happen to me."

"Then go and send my good wishes."

With a smile, Ian waved his hand in a circle above his head, and just like that, he was gone.

Darca smiled, "the man I met is no longer, now stands a powerful wizard. Children, it is time to feed." All her children gathered around and one by one Darca fed them. The only thing missing was her mate.

When Ian arrived with Drago and the other dragons he couldn't believe his eyes. It was a castle from fairytales, white with high steeples on each corner around the castle and there was a large white wall with a massive drawbridge, and underneath was a moat. Yes, a moat. Atop the castle on all four corners was the flag of a red dragon with a lightning bolt through the center. It was magnificent to see.

"Ian, tis your name now?" asked Merlin.

Ian turned when he heard his name, and what he saw coming to him was a tall man with a long silver robe and long silver hair, a beard, and a mustache, and to Ian's surprise, he was wearing a pointed hat. "You are Merlin, aren't you," Ian said, looking at him with starry eyes.

Merlin smiled, "yes, and you are the wizard I once knew as Caldif."

"Yes. I can't believe it's you. It's really you. You have been a tale told…a myth. No one believed you truly existed. Of course, no one believed dragons existed, and yet, they do."

Merlin belted out a laugh, one that shook the ground. "Ian, thee are humorous. I nay one to be worshiped. I am only a man."

"Only a man! You are the most powerful wizard of all time," Ian said with excitement.

Placing his hand on Ian's shoulder, "nay, I am one of two now. Thee have great powers, ones thee are not fully aware of yet."

"Yeah, I am still learning my powers. One day, I will have silver hair and a beard like you."

"Come, would thy like to meet King Arthur, your new king?"

"Would I. He is another I cannot wait to meet. Please, show me the way."

"Do thee remember how to greet a king such as Arthur?" Merlin asked.

"Well, no. I haven't had much dealings with royalty."

"Well, when we walk into the throne room, thee will wait until I motion for thee to come forward. I will go to King Arthur to inform him of who thee is, and once I motion for thee to come forward, thou will approach slowly with thy head down. Once you are a few feet from the throne, thee will bow until King Arthur ask thee to rise. Once you rise, do naught look him directly in his eyes. Thee are not to be so familiar with him."

"Boy, I am not sure if I am ready for this."

"Seek thy memory of who thy was before, Caldif met many kings and queens during his life."

Ian did as Merlin asked, and he did, he found the information he was looking for. He stood straight and said, "I am ready."

With that, Merlin took Ian to meet King Arthur.

When Ian and Merlin arrived and entered the throne room, it was magnificent. The ceilings were as high as the eyes could see and there were windows on the right side that filled one wall with gothic windows that were framed with gold. There were white marble columns with gold leaves that decorated the top and bottom of the columns, lining the path that led to the throne. The throne itself was a simple, yet elegant gold chair that sat on a block made of white marble. Even the entire floor and walls were made of marble with splashes of gold. The room was very luxurious, one made for kings and queens.

Ian turned to Merlin, "this is the most beautiful throne room I have ever seen. Of course, it is the only throne room I have ever seen," Ian said, giving Merlin a wide smile.

Merlin returned the smile, "wait here while I inform King Arthur thee are here." Ian nodded and Merlin continued to the throne.

"Your majesty," Merlin said, as he bowed to King Arthur.

"Merlin, thee know you do naught need to bow to me. Thee are naught only my sorcerer, but my friend."

"I thank thee, but tis naught proper naught to bow to thee."

Shaking his head, "very well. What thou need of me?"

"Your majesty, I would like to introduce thee to a young wizard, who once, many years ago was my closest friend, who has been reborn into this new life."

King Arthur looked toward the back by the doors at Ian standing there with his head down waiting to be called forth. "That young man is thy old friend?" he asked with a questionable eye.

Merlin smiled, "tis true. I have told thee wizard can live many years and when they leave this world they can be reborn."

"Thee did say so, but I have naught seen it until now," King Arthur said looking at Ian. "Well, I am interested in meeting this old friend reborn. Bring him forward."

Merlin turned to Ian and nodded his head, indicating he may approach.

When Ian received the nod from Merlin, he knew it was time to meet Arthur…Arthur, the legendary king people believed to be a myth. Swallowing the lump in his throat, *well, it looks like it's time to meet the legend,* he thought as

137

he headed to the throne where King Arthur sat. Once Ian was a few feet away he stopped.

"So, thee are Merlin's old friend reborn?" King Arthur asked.

"Yes, Your Majesty."

"Well, what shall I do with thee," King Arthur asked looking at Merlin with a smile on his face. Then turned back to Ian. "What proof do thee have thee are the old wizard from a time long ago?" he asked.

"Your Majesty, what proof can I give you, but that I am here," Ian said.

Arthur placed his hand on his chin, thinking of what would be the perfect proof, and when he came to it he snapped his fingers. "Merlin, do thee remember when we went to Cardiff and thee introduced me to thy friend Caldif."

"Ah, I do, and tis a good proof. If Ian was naught my friend, he would naught remember," Merlin said, turning to Ian."

Ian was watching King Arthur and Merlin talk about him and wondered if he would be able to recall a memory from that time.

"Ian can thee search thy memory for the time we came to visit thee in Cardiff," Merlin asked.

"I don't know Merlin, but I will try," Ian said as he searched his memory, searching trying to find that which included Merlin and King Arthur, and after a few moments it came to him. Merlin and King Arthur rode on horseback side by side into the village near Badon Mount after a battle looking for rest, food, drink, and women. Ian smiled. "I remember when you and Merlin rode into my village after the battle of Badon Mount looking for food, drink, and…women," he said smiling at the memory, "and I participated in those celebrations," he said showing his white teeth.

King Arthur burst out laughing, oh, he remembered those days, "well, then thee can only be Caldif," he said, as he moved from his throne to walk over to Ian. He placed his hand on Ian's shoulders, "old friend of Merlin, there is no need for thee to look down. Rise thy head and look up at my face, as thee has earned the right to do so all those years ago."

Ian, still smiling, did as King Arthur said, and to look at the great man himself, was a wonderful gift. "Thank you, King Arthur," Ian said.

After, King Arthur sent word that the celebration shall commence in three days hence, and when it did, the three celebrated until the sun began to rise on the next day. After everyone from all around, humans, creatures, fairies, and dragons attended King Arthur's coronation and accepted him as the world's first and only king. It was a celebration like no other, one only written in fairytale books.

"Beladore," Queen Allabella said, "why did ye no go with the other dragons?"

"Tis naught my time anymore. Tis best to remain here," said Beladore.

"Yer time may be gone, but ye are no forgotten. Ye are the leader of those dragons, and as the leader, ye should be with them."

"Nay, another will take my place, as it should be."

"Then will ye leave to the other world?"

"Nay, although I should, I am not ready. Tis place is what I know. This new world thee speak of is strange to me."

"Darca and Tlachtga are still alive and in this new world. No, tis no the world ye remember, tis a new world that would be better than ye remember."

Beladore thought of everything the queen said, but he was still not sure if he was ready to return to such a world. Yes, he would love to see Darca again and her children, after all, it was many millennia since he last saw her. Turning to leave, "I will think on what thee said," he said, as he left to fly the night sky.

How can I leave such a place? This place that Queen Allabella created is more beautiful than the one I left. How can I leave this place," he thought. Beladore thought back to how he came to this place after he woke from his long sleep, and found all his brethren were gone. They were either asleep or here in the Fairy Realm.

Beladore searched and searched to find other dragons to no avail, and when he heard the stories being told, that hundred years ago all the dragons vanished from the land. Unsure what happened, but heard some went to the Fairy Realm, and after a time, he didn't want to remain in a world alone, so he searched for a way to be with his brethren. Through his search, he learned there was only one who could help him. Beladore looked to the night sky and then called the name Cathbad, the druid from the realm of light. After a few moments, there was a shimmer of light and then there was Cathbad standing in the meadow right below him. Beladore wasted no time and quickly went to Cathbad and landed directly in front of him.

"Beladore, it is a pleasure to see you again."

Beladore bowed his head, "and thou. Tis been a long time since our last meeting."

"That has. Why have you called on me?" Cathbad asked looking around. "Tell me great one, why have you called on me?"

"I know naught of what thee know of what happened to my brethren, but most have gone to the Fairy Realm, from what I heard and the other's I —"

Cathbad interrupted Beladore, "they are only asleep. They went to sleep until the people were ready to accept them again, but my friend, I am sorry to say, it will be a very long time before that happens," Cathbad said with sadness.

Although it sadden Beladore, he was pleased to hear his brethren were only asleep and not dead. "Tis relieves my heart to know this. Thank thee Cathbad."

"Now, tell me why you called on me. What can I do to help you?"

"Will thou send me to the Fairy Realm?"

"I am sorry Beladore, I do not know where it is, so I cannot send you there, but I can call on Queen Allabella and she can open the door to her realm.

"I thank thee Cathbad."

Cathbad quickly reached for Queen Allabella and when he made contact, *Your Majesty, can you come to the Earth Realm?*

Tis a pleasure to hear from ye, Cathbad, but I can no open the realm without the power of a powerful wizard or dragon.

I am with Beladore, he and I, along with you can open the door.

Beladore! Tis wonderful news to know he has woken.

Yes, and he wishes to come to your realm.

Then he is very welcome. I will go to the oak tree here and ye and Beladore need to find one there. Once ye are there, call on me and together we will open the door to my realm.

Beladore and Cathbad searched and found an oak tree only a few yards away, and once they were there they called on Queen Allabella again.

I am here Cathbad, then together they used their powers and opened the door to their realm, and standing on the other side was Queen Allabella.

"Beladore, tis a pleasure to see ye again."

"And thee, Queen Allabella."

"Beladore, ye are very welcome to my realm."

"Thank thee, Queen Allabella," Beladore said turning to Cathbad. "Thank thee, Cathbad, do thee want to come with me?"

"No Beladore. Once you are through, I will return to my realm. If you need me again, you only have to call on me."

Beladore nodded his head and after Beladore went through the door and it closed behind him, he returned to the realm of light.

Ronny Whitman

Chapter 10

Everyone and creature gathered at Tempe Town Lake to meet the newborn dragons. Ian was dressed in his wizard robe, with his staff in hand as his arms were stretched out to his sides. "Here, as all of you have gathered, I introduce you to the children of Darca, the first dragons born in many millennia."

One by one the baby dragons appeared in the sky, and everyone cheered in welcome, and once the dragons made their debut, a celebration reigned on for five days, and on the final day, a new dragon appeared in the sky.

It was Darca who saw him first. "Ian, it is him."

"Who?" Ian asked, turning towards the new dragon that was flying towards them.

In tears and with a crack in her voice, "my mate. It's my mate, Ian."

Ian was surprised, yet not, he had expected this was the surprise Queen Allabella mentioned, but he also wondered why it took him so long to arrive, yet pleased and happy that after all these years – centuries, Darca's mate was alive and returning to be by her side.

"My mate, thy live?" he said with surprise and joy.

"Yes, and you, you are alive. Where have you been all this time?"

"I was in the Fairy Realm, and when the Fairy Queen delivered the news that dragons have returned to the world, we sought permission to return and when the door between our two worlds opened, we came through. After returning to this world, I went to the place that was once my home, and after meeting the other dragons and learning of what happened, and the ancient who made it possible, I immediately set out to find…I did not know it was thee."

"My mate, I have believed you dead once the dragons woke and you were not among them. It gives me great joy to see you are alive. Come, you must meet your children," she said with a smile.

Darca called to her children and when they arrived, "children, I want you to meet your father."

The children went to the male dragon and smelled him and immediately recognized him as their father and flew around him with joy.

Darca," Ian called out.

Darca turned to Ian, "Ian, please meet my mate. His name is Tlachtga," she said.

Ian gave Darca a wide smile, and bowed as he said, "it is a great honor to meet you."

"The honor is mine, wizard," Tlachtga said, bowing his head in return.

The night went on celebrating the joy of the new and old life coming together, connecting two worlds as one. Life on Terra was one with the greatest happiness and joy the planet has ever seen. Finally, there was peace in the world. Then suddenly, there was another dragon approaching.

Darca saw him first, "Tlachtga, look, another dragon, who could that be."

Tlachtga turned to the dragon approaching and immediately knew who it was. "Wait, thy…you will see."

Once the new dragon was closer, Darca immediately recognized him, and she turned to her mate with shock. "Beladore. Beladore, he is alive."

Tlachtga smiled, "yes. He was with us in the Fairy Realm but stayed behind. I wonder how he is here now.

Once Beladore reached Darca and Tlachtga, he landed directly in front of them and bowed his head, "Darca and Tlachtga, tis nice to see thee again."

Darca could not believe the ancient who was the leader of the dragons during her time was still alive and well. "Beladore, I cannot believe you are alive and here," she said with excitement.

"Tis a pleasure to see thee as well, Darca. After the dragons left, I found myself alone and after a time, and after talking with Queen Allabella, I decided it was time to return to this realm. When I went to Queen Allabella to make my request, first she said it was impossible, and then she called on me and told me tis possible and if I wish it, I could return this night. Well, I wished it and after she reached out to Ian, the door opened and here I am."

Darca and Tlachtga looked at each other and were amazed that the oldest of all dragons, a true ancient was still alive and with them once again.

Darca bowed her head, "then thee should be the leader of all dragons. I relinquish my role willingly."

"Nay, Darca. Thee return the dragons and fairies to the world, thee have earned thy honor to be leader."

Shaking her head, "nay, tis belongs to thee."

"Nay, Darca, it belongs to thee," he said and bowed his head out of respect.

Darca knew there would be no changing Beladore's mind, so Darca bowed her head and in return, "then I accept, and your approval means everything to me. Thank you, Beladore. If I may, there…I am sure there will be times I will need your counsel, will you be my advisor?"

Beladore bowed, "it would be my honor."

"Come, meet our children," said Tlachtga.

Tlachtga and Darca introduced Beladore to their children and their children went easily to Beladore and played with him, and all was right in the world.

Three months since Tlachtga returned, Darca and their children were flying in the night sky beneath the glow of the moon and stars. "Look at them, they are the best we have created. They are you and me. They have grown so much since I arrived. Do you think they will fly as fast as I?" Tlachtga asked.

"Or I," said Darca.

"Shall we put it to the test as we once did to see who is faster?" he asked.

Darca smiled and nodded her head, and before she knew it, they were racing across the sky filled with joy and happiness they never believed was possible.

Ian. Ian.

Queen Allabella, how may I be of assistance?

Ian, I just learned that when we let the dragons through the door into yer realm, an evil fae snuck through. I need yer help to find him and return him to my realm.

Queen Allabella, I will do everything I can to find this fae and return him to your realm. What can you tell me about this fae?

His name is Finn, and he has the power to turn one's will into his own. He is very dangerous Ian, very, and it will take ye and the power of the dragons and…I heard Merlin has awakened…call on him for help. He helped to deal with the evil Fae before.

I understand and I will do all I can to return this Finn to your realm.

Thank ye, Ian, and good luck.

Without waiting, Ian reached out to Darca and Tlachtga. *Darca, Tlachtga, I must speak with you at once. Can we meet?*

Ian, yes, of course. Where? asked Darca.

At Dragon Valley and now if you can.

At first, there was silence, which Ian believed Darca and Tlachtga were talking among each other.

Ian, we will meet you now.

Thank you, Darca.

When Darca and Tlachtga arrived at Tempe Town Lake, they found Ian standing alone near the meadow waiting for them. Then, just as they landed, another man appeared with long silver-white hair and a beard, wearing a pointed hat.

That must be the wizard Merlin Ian told us about, Darca said.

Yes. I wonder what has happened.

After Darca and Tlachtga landed, "good evening Ian," Tlachtga said, bowing his head.

"Good evening Darca and Tlachtga, this is Merlin, the wizard I told you about," Ian said, turning to Merlin.

"Tis a pleasure to meet thee. Tis been long since I have seen thy kind," said Merlin.

"We have heard of thee from Queen Allabella," Darca said turning to Tlachtga, "and my mate has lived in her realm for many centuries."

Merlin turned to Tlachtga, "thee know the stories then?" he asked.

Tlachtga smiled, "yes. Many."

Darca looked at her mate, *you did not tell me these stories?* she asked.

I am sorry, but I was focused on being with you again and our children, Tlachtga said.

147

Darca and Tlachtga turned to Ian and Merlin, "tell us what reason you called us here?" Darca asked.

"Well, I received an urgent message from Queen Allabella. She informed me an evil fae named Finn managed to sneak through the door between her and our realm. He has the ability to manipulate one's mind."

Darca turned to Tlachtga, *Queen Allabella and I knew of a fae like this, but she destroyed him that day we went to the village along with the others.*

You did, but a few escaped and when Queen Allabella learned this, she did everything she could to stop him…them. Turning to Merlin, *Merlin was the wizard who helped stop him, and once he was captured Queen Allabella took him to the Fairy Realm where she designed a place with a protective shield preventing them from using their powers, which allowed them to live free, but something must have gone wrong.*

"What? I know you are talking, please tell us what you know?" asked Ian.

"Sorry, Ian. I was just informing Darca of this fae you spoke of. Merlin knows of him, and he and Queen Allabella worked together to capture him and his followers, but not before he managed to kill many humans or destroyed their minds forever. He is very evil. He can manipulate any mind, human, fairy, and dragon."

"Yes, tis true. If Queen Allabella created this protective shield that prevented them from using their powers, then we must know what happened," Merlin said, turning to Ian, "we must open the doorway and speak with Queen Allabella and find out how he managed to get free. By now, she would have learned what happened."

"Very well," said Ian.

Together, Ian and Merlin used their powers and within a few moments Queen Allabella was coming through the door between their realm and the Fairy Realm.

"Tis a pleasure to see ye again Merlin and Ian," then she turned to Darca and Tlachtga, "oh Darca, my friend, tis good to see ye again. I have missed our times together."

Darca was full of joy at seeing Queen Allabella and her friend again. "Oh, Your Majesty, I have missed you very much. It is an honor," bowing her head, "to see you again."

"We must find time to spend together once this is over."

"Oh yes, and you must meet," turning to Tlachtga, "our children."

"Aye, aye, that I shall. Now, we must discuss why ye brought me here."

"Yes, Queen Allabella, tell us more of this Finn who escaped. We need to know how and what he plans on doing?" asked Merlin.

"This Finn is a fae from the time when Darca and I went to a village to find evil fae, tis believed all were destroyed by my hand, but he and two others escaped. When I learned of this, it was a thousand years later and this Finn had done much damage. This was also when I met Merlin, the first wizard. He was a druid from the realm of light who came through and was able to keep his powers instead of them dwelling with time. Tis rare, but possible. With Merlin's strong powers and mine, we were able to trap Finn in a shield, where I took him and his followers to the Fairy Realm, and there, several days from my castle, on land where I created a shield around the area that prevented them from using their powers and breaking through the shield, but something must have gone wrong. If there was a little crack, it would have been enough to restore one's

Ronny Whitman

power. I believe I know how he escaped. That small crack was enough to manipulate one young dragon's mind. I learned that a young dragon, no more than a hundred years old ventured out to that side of the realm, curious about the evil fae…from the stories he heard growing up. This child dragon was the one to help Finn escape. Of course, not realizing he was helping him."

Concerned, "Queen Allabella, who was this dragon? Who are his parents?" Tlachtga asked.

Queen Allabella turned to Tlachtga with sorrow in her eyes, "it was Gildore, son of Rango and Tya."

This surprised Tlachtga. He knew Gildore, and he would never do anything that would bring harm to anyone. He must have been manipulated to go to where the evil fae was. "No, Gildore would never go against your law. He had to have been lured to go there, but how? Is it possible Finn's power was enough to reach Gildore so far away?"

"I no naught. Tis possible, but the crack would have been there for many moons for Finn's power to be that strong. I would send guards to check the boundary to ensure there were no cracks."

"Is it possible when they did, with that crack, Finn could have manipulated the guards so that they found no break or damage to the shield," asked Merlin.

"Aye, tis possible. Tis means Finn's power was greater than I believed. If so, tis my fault he escaped."

"No," Tlachtga said firmly, "it is no one's fault but Finn's. Is it possible Finn is still using Gildore?" he asked with concern.

"Tis possible. Have ye seen Gildore since he's been here?" Queen Allabella asked.

"He and his parents were here, but they went to live in Scotland," said Darca.

"If Gildore is still controlled by Finn, he will go there to use Gildore to help bring destruction to Scotland and anywhere else he chooses to go. This is very dangerous. We must get Gildore away from Finn to save him and break the hold Finn has on him. If we can get to him, I can remove the hold and protect his mind, while Merlin and Ian use their powers to trap Finn, then…we will need Beladore's power along with Darca, Tlachtga, Merlin, and Ian to destroy Finn and his followers for good. Tis the only way to protect the world. Tis must be done."

"Then we need to call for Beladore to come here," said Darca, but did not wait for an answer, she immediately called for Beladore to come to Dragon Valley.

When Beladore arrived, "Queen Allabella, tis a pleasure to see thee again. Why are thee here?" he asked with surprise. Looking around he knew something serious was happening. "Tell me, what has happened?"

"Finn escaped my realm," said Queen Allabella.

"Tis naught possible."

"Aye, tis true. We need yer help to stop him for good."

"Then thee shall have it. What tis the plan?"

Darca, Tlachtga, Queen Allabella, and Merlin relayed what their plan was – they were going to travel to Scotland, find Finn, and Ian and Merlin are going to use their powers to trap Finn and his followers and destroy them for good. Once this is done, it should break the hold Finn has on Gildore, but Queen Allabella will ensure he is free from Finn for good.

"If Finn makes Gildore use his powers to destroy humans, it will be like it was before. I can naught allow this to happen. We will save Gildore not destroy him," said Beladore firmly.

151

"Aye, I no believe we will. Cillian joined with an evil wizard and practiced dark magic, tis why it was difficult to change him. There is no evil wizard or dark magic influencing Gildore, tis I will be able to save him," Queen Allabella said firmly and with sympathy. She knows how difficult it was for Beladore to destroy Cillian, and she will not allow that to happen again. Not this time.

"Then, shall we go?" said Beladore.

"Yes, but we must take care of our children first," said Darca.

"Gildore's parents will care for your children while we go to save their son," said Beladore.

"Yes, they will not harm our children. They are good and honorable dragons and parents," said Tlachtga.

"If you believe this mate, then I shall trust them with our children."

Tlachtga called for Gildore's parents and when they arrived he explained what happened as did Queen Allabella, and although fearful for their son, they agreed to remain and take care of Tlachtga and Darca's children. Once everything was in order, Merlin used his powers to take everyone to Scotland, and in a short time, a tornado formed around them, and within moments they were transported to Scotland.

Ronny Whitman

Chapter 11

When they arrived in Scotland, they were on the Island of Skye. "We should change our appearance into one of the locals," said Queen Allabella.

"Yes, let us all change our appearance. Ian, have you learned how to do this yet?" asked Merlin.

"No, I am sorry, I have not."

"Tis fine, I will do it for thee and Merlin," said Queen Allabella and just as she was about to cast her spell, Merlin stopped her.

"Your Majesty, since we do naught know where Finn is, we can naught take the chance he will since thy powers. I will create a shield around all of us that should prevent Finn from sensing thy power. We will know within moments if he did."

Thank ye, Merlin," said Queen Allabella, and within seconds, Merlin and Ian were Scottish Highlanders of old and there was no sign of Finn. "Ah, tis appear yer shield worked."

Merlin smiled and nodded his head in agreement.

"Tis amazing…my speech, tis of Scottish," Ian said with amazement.

"Aye, tis best to be and speak as Scottish," said Merlin with a smile.

Just then, Darca, Tlachtga, and Beladore were also Scottish men and women of old. "Let us go south, but we must walk and no use our powers. Finn will sense mine and I am sure he will sense yers as well. While Merlin's shield was around us, I created a protective shield around yer mind so he can no use ye. If ye feel the push of his powers, ye must pretend to be affected or he will know ye are

Ronny Whitman

protected. If tis becomes too dangerous, I will use my powers to remove ye from where ye are."

Everyone nodded in agreement and began to head out once Queen Allabella, through Merlin so she would not be detected, used her powers to locate Finn. "He is four leagues away."

"Can he since yer powers so close?" Merlin asked.

"Only if I use them, tis possible, but I will no use my powers unless I have no choice," said Queen Allabella.

"Leagues? What are leagues?" Ian asked.

"Tis what ye call miles," Darca said.

"How many miles in a league?" Ian asked.

Darca had to search Ian's mind for that information, "ah, tis twelve of yer miles."

"Twelve miles! Are ye kidding me," then remembering where and who he was – after all, as a wizard from his past life he walked many miles. It's how things were done then. Ian looked around to those who were with him – *these are the ones who lived in those times, how am I to complain, after all, haven't I been forced to walk since the war? No fool, ye used a horse and walked when ye had to, but only a few miles.* Ian pulled his shoulders back and with more confidence, "forgive me. Walking will no be a problem."

Darca laughed, "Ian, of course, ye can walk twelve miles. When we walked yer downtown Phoenix, we walked several miles. This is no different."

"Aye, ye are right. I also pulled up memories of my past life as a wizard…reminding me of the many miles he had to walk…I can do this."

"Ian, do the people of this time no walk anywhere?" Merlin asked, with curiosity.

"Well, only for pleasure. We usually ride horses or drive a car if we have to go more than a couple of miles."

"People today have become lazy," Merlin said with disgust. "Ian, ye are a wizard now, and there are times ye will be required to do things without yer powers," Merlin said, then, "tis time we be on our way."

"Ye are right. Sorry, Merlin. I must seem like a weak wizard compared to ye," Ian said with disappointment.

Merlin put his hand on Ian's shoulder, "tis alright Ian. Ye knew no better. Ye will learn," he said, sighing.

"Thank ye, Merlin. We best be going, aye. Hearing myself talk," he said, then change the mood, "tis sounds so strange."

Merlin and the others laughed, as they headed out to find Finn.

Finn was standing on what the Scots of this time call Fairy Glen. It's a path in a spiral shape, going from small to large until it ends with small stones. Finn laughed, *tis silly humans,* he thought shaking his head.

Then, out of know where, Finn felt power coming from the circle, *power? How tis possible?* he thought and then had an idea. *I can use my power with this power and possibly learn where the wizard hid his dark magic book.* Finn moved to the center of the circle and put out his arms as he looked at the sky, connecting with the power of the stones and the energy of the earth. Finn used all his powers to push out his senses searching for the dark powers of the magic book of where it was hidden.

As Finn did this, miles and miles away, Queen Allabella picked up the surge in power and she quickly came to a halt. "We have a problem. Finn is using his powers and I feel tis for no good. Merlin, if I use my powers to see what

155

Finn is doing, he will know I am here. Can ye use yer powers to learn what he is doing?"

"Aye, I can." With that, Merlin closed his eyes and expanded his senses searching for Finn through the use of his powers, and just as he had it, he lost it. "Ian, my power is not strong enough. I need yer power combined with mine."

"Tell me what to do?"

"Just focus yer energy and direct it to me. I will take yer energy and combine it with mine."

As Ian focused on his energy, he could feel Merlin pulling it from him and combining it with his own.

After Merlin combined Ian's energy with his, he again sent out his senses in search of Finn, and when he found him, he could not believe what he was doing, "tis no possible," Merlin said with shock.

"Merlin, what do ye see," asked Queen Allabella with concern,

"Finn is trying to find the evil book of magic from the dark wizard."

Everyone was shocked and started voicing their concern, then Queen Allabella turned and put up her hand to hush everyone. "Merlin, is this possible?"

Merlin nodded, "aye, tis is. I took the book after I destroyed the evil wizard and hid it in a cave near Cardiff," Merlin said.

"That is in Wales, but I no naught if tis still there since England was destroyed," said Ian.

"Aye, tis possible, but we must find the book and destroy it before Finn does," said Merlin.

"Can we get there using our magic without Finn knowing?" Ian asked.

Merlin looked around at everyone and then at Queen Allabella, "what do ye think Queen Allabella?" Merlin asked.

"Tis possible he will sense our power, especially mine. Merlin can ye use yer power to transport us all there without Finn knowing?" she asked.

"With the amount of magic I must use, tis no guarantee he will no sense my power."

"Is there another way?" asked Darca.

"No, if we want to beat Finn there. I am sure he will use his powers to travel, but he must find the location of the book first," Merlin said.

"We must go now and take our chance," said Queen Allabella.

"Darca and Tlachtga, can ye use yer powers to see if ye can sense if Finn picks up our powers?" Merlin asked.

Darca turned to Tlachtga, *what do ye think?*

Aye, I believe tis possible.

Together, Darca and Tlachtga nodded, and with that, they sent out their senses until they picked up Finn's and then let Merlin know, "now. Tis now while he is focused on finding the book," said Darca.

With that, Merlin used his powers and within seconds there were standing outside the opening of a cave.

"Wow, that was amazing," Ian said.

Everyone turned and smiled at Ian. "What?" Ian asked.

Darca and Merlin were shaking their heads, "tis a young pup is he no," said Merlin to Darca.

Darca burst out laughing, "aye, he is that."

Ian looked at them both, "ha ha ha, okay, ye have yer fun."

"Aye," said Merlin.

"Merlin, how far in the cave is the book?" asked Queen Allabella.

"It's very deep with many safeguards. Tis best I go in alone and when I return with the book, we will destroy it once and for all," Merlin said.

As Finn was focusing his senses using the power of the stone circle, the energy of the earth, and his own powers, he felt he was getting close to where the book was, and as he got closer, he sensed another power, one, possibly as great or greater this his. "No, tis no possible. Merlin can no be alive. If he gets to the book before I, he will destroy it." Finn wasted no time, he increased his powers and worked as quickly as possible to find the book before Merlin. By the time Finn found the location, he sensed he was already too late, and without further thought, Finn focused his power and transported himself to where Merlin was, and when he arrived, he could not believe what he saw – there were, what appears to be four humans standing at the edge of a cave. *Who are these people and what are they doing here where I sensed Merlin,* he thought, looking around to see where Merlin was, but when he couldn't find him, *he must be inside the cave. That must be where the book is. I can no let Merlin get the book.* With that, Finn stepped out from behind the tree where he was hiding and approached the group of humans.

It was Ian who first noticed Finn, *Darca, don't turn around, but Finn is coming directly at us.*

How do ye know tis him?

I saw his image in Merlin's mind when we merged our powers.

Darca immediately reached out to Queen Allabella, *Yer Majesty, Finn is approaching us. It doesn't appear he knows who we are, as I no sense any ill intent towards us.*

Our disguise is good enough to full a fae such as he, but – turning her mind to everyone, *do nothing to give away that we are anything but mere humans. He doesn't sense we are anything but. Be ready, if we no give him the answer he seeks, he will try to force ye to tell him what he wants to know. Once ye feel the push to his question, answer it as we look to him, that we are mere humans hiking and considering entering the cave to explore.*

Everyone agreed and prepared themselves for what was to come. Queen Allabella reached to Merlin. *Finn is here. At the moment he no believes we are anything but humans. Be careful when ye return.*

I sense him. Once I have the book, I will return, and once I leave the cave, erect a shield around all of us and hold it until we can destroy the book.

I do no know if I can hold the shield and our image as well as destroy the book.

Darca and Tlachtga, can ye hold the shield while we put our powers together to destroy the book before Finn can break through? Merlin asked.

Darca and Tlachtga looked at each other, *aye, we can. Aye, Merlin, we can.*

Just then Finn was only a few feet away, appearing as a human male instead of a Fae. "Good day. How are ye doing this wonderful day," Finn asked, as he sends out his senses to determine who these people were, but all he found were four humans, which caused him to smile within.

Ian was the one to respond, "aye, we are. We were just discussing about exploring," turning toward the cave entrance, "this cave," he said.

"Oh aye, well, then ye should be glad I arrived in time," Finn said, nodding toward the cave, "tis a dangerous cave. Ye will bring yerself to harm if ye enter."

Ian showed surprise, yet with a sense of relief, which pleased Finn. "Oh aye, if tis true, "turning to the others, "tis best we do no enter."

Darca now had to play her part, "oh aye, ye are then a coward if ye are afraid of a little cave," she said.

Tlachtga reigned in, "aye, tis true. Ye are a coward if ye no want to go. If tis so, ye can stay and watch our things while we go to explore."

To hear this, worried Finn and he quickly sought the mind of the male who spoke, and when he reached his mind, he saw a man eager to explore a cave of wonder and nothing more.

When Tlachtga felt Finn attempt to touch his mind, he gave him what he wanted him to see, a man eager to explore a cave.

"Well, if ye desire this, then ye are welcome to explore, Will ye mine if I join ye?" Finn asked.

Although Finn asked to join them, at the same time he was planting the seed that they needed to leave and explore another cave. When they all filled this push, they knew they had to play along until Merlin arrived.

Merlin, Finn is pushing for us to leave. If we no do as he asks, he will know he has no power over us, said Queen Allabella.

Play along, I will be there in a moment. I have the book. Darca, Tlachtga, Ian, be ready. When you see me, Darca and Tlachtga will raise the shield and hold it while we work together to destroy this book. I will give ye the words to say and we will need to say them together.

"Hey, I think we should go to another cave. This one doesn't seem that interesting," Ian said.

Everyone said at once, "oh aye, I agree."

Just then, everyone began to pick up their backs and as they were placing them on their backs Merlin appeared at the entrance of the cave, "Now," he said.

With that, a shield was raised, and when Finn since the surge of power he immediately lashed out but found an impenetrable shield, which angered him. He called up all his powers and threw it at the shield knowing with enough power the shield will collapse.

"Quickly, we don't have much time before he breaks through the shield," said Darca.

Merlin quickly sent the words into everyone's mind and began to chant as he held the book with his mind in the air, but out of sight from Finn. "Tute tata tute tata tute tata," they repeated over and over again, and while they were doing this, the book began to smoke, and after several minutes, the shield around them began to waiver.

"We must speed up the chant and destroy the book before the shield fails," said Merlin.

And everyone poured all their power and energy they had that wasn't used to hold the shield to destroy the book and before they knew it, the book burst into flames and within seconds, it was all but ashes floating in the air.

"Now!" yelled Queen Allabella, and they all turned their power on Finn.

To Finn's shock, their power was greater than his, and he tried to run – to use his power to escape, but to his horror, he was held in place by a power greater than his – Queen of the Fae.

When Finn looked at what were humans, he saw the Fae Queen, two dragons, a human man, and the most powerful wizard of all time, Merlin. He was angered that he had been fooled and knew there was nothing he could do, and within a few moments he began to tear away, piece by piece, and before he was gone forever, "ye think with me gone, tis over," he said with an evil laugh, "aye, but ye will be wrong. There are other's I have already manipulated to do my bidding, and although I will be gone, they will remain and do what I have programmed them to do," he said and then he was no more.

Once Finn was gone, "is what he says possible?" Ian asked.

Queen Allabella quickly used her powers to search for any others out there that may have been influenced by Finn, and to her shock, he was not lying. Without waiting, she quickly returned each of the human's mind that Finn infected back to their natural human ones, and then she searched for any other fae that might be out there, and to her relief there was none.

"Tis over," she said with glee.

Everyone was relieved and Ian jumped up with joy that they defeated a powerful fae like Finn. "So, what do we do now?" Ian asked.

"We return to our lives. I will return to my realm and ye will return to your lives as it was," said Queen Allabella.

And that is just what happened. Merlin opened the doorway and Queen Allabella bid them goodbye and returned to her realm. After Merlin returned to King Arthur's side, Ian, Darca, and Tlachtga returned to Phoenix and their lives.

It has been ten years since the evil fae was destroyed and the world together were living in peace, a peace the world has never seen since the time Darca had lived. For

162

Beladore, he finally decided to leave this world for the next, and before he did, he ensured Darca had all his memories and powers that were given to him when he became leader, as the new leader of the dragons. She became a great leader, greater than any other, and the children were loved and treated with the status which had been bestowed on them as the children of Darca.

For Queen Allabella, after a time, did the only thing she could, she destroyed all the evil fae – the Unseelie, and open the door and kept it open between the Fairy Realm and the earth realm. Once again, humans, fairies, and dragons were living together in harmony. This also allowed the druids of the realm of light to once again come to the earth's realm to pick one human to hold all the powers of the druids, and after proving his worth, they chose Ian. Ian was now like Merlin, one of the most powerful wizards of all time. Earth was finally at peace, living in harmony for the first time in thousands of years.

The End.

Ronny Whitman

9 7989 99428 7033